Library of Congress Cataloging-in-Publication Data

Conkling, Winifred.
Sylvia and Aki / by Winifred Conkling. — 1st ed.
    p. cm.
Summary: At the start of World War II, Japanese American third-grader
Aki and her family are sent to an internment camp in Poston, Arizona,
while Mexican American third-grader Sylvia's family leases their Orange
County, California, farm and begins a fight to stop school segregation.
1. Race relations—Fiction. 2. Segregation in education—Fiction.
. Japanese Americans—Evacuation and relocation, 1942-1945—
iction. 4. Mexican Americans—Fiction. 5. Farm life—California—
ction. 6. Poston Relocation Center (Ariz.)—Fiction. 7. Orange County
alif.)—History—20th century—Fiction.] I. Title.
Z7.C76182Syl 2011
ic]—dc22
                        2010024182

N 978-1-58246-337-7 (hardcover)
N 978-1-58246-397-1 (Gibraltar lib. bdg.)

ted in U.S.A.

gn by Colleen Cain
set in Adrianna, Classical Garamond, Florens, Lomba,
Artcraft, and P22 Garamouche Ornaments

5 6 – 16 15 14 13 12 11

dition

Sylvia
&
Aki

WINIFRED CONKLIN

TRICYCLE PRESS
Berkeley

For Sylvia Mendez and
Aki Munemitsu Nakauchi;
this is your story.

CONTENTS

A NOTE ABOUT WORD CHOICE

Today we use the terms "Mexican American" and "Japanese American" when referring to United States citizens of Mexican and Japanese descent. In the 1940s, however, these people were commonly called "Mexicans" and "Japanese," regardless of citizenship. The term "Mexican" was also used to describe people from all Spanish-speaking countries, not just those from Mexico. In keeping with the language usage of the period, this book uses the words "Mexican" and "Japanese," although the author recognizes that many of the people involved were U.S. citizens.

Sylvia called her parents "Mom" and "Dad" and Aki referred to "Mom" and "Pop." They used these classic American names rather than *Mami* and *Papi* or *Okaasan* and *Otousan* in an attempt to assimilate, or blend, into American culture.

Last, in the city of Westminster, California, where much of this story takes place, Westminster Main School was also known as the 17th Street School. Sylvia and Aki remember it as "Westminster School," and that is how it is referred to in the book.

PART I

California and Arizona
1941

CHAPTER 1

He who doesn't look ahead remains behind.
—MEXICAN PROVERB

Sylvia
Westminster, California

Sylvia Mendez imagined her first day of third grade at Westminster School. She would use her freshly sharpened yellow pencils to write her name in cursive at the top of her worksheets. Her just-out-of-the-shoebox black Mary Janes would glide across the polished linoleum of the hallway. At the end of the day, she would come home and her father would hug her and ask, "What did you learn today?" Then she would tell him about her teacher and her classmates and everything else.

Sylvia never imagined the one thing that actually happened even before her first day of school: she was turned away.

Summer vacation was nearly over. It was the morning Sylvia was to register for school. She rode with her aunt Soledad, her two brothers, and her cousins in the backseat of her family's blue Pontiac sedan, watching orange groves and fields of lima beans, sugar beets, and asparagus rush by. The flat southern California landscape stretched to the mountains, one farm after another, each a distinct pattern of green stripes.

We have a farm, Sylvia thought. *For the first time, our very own farm.*

Sylvia's father had worked as a field hand on other people's farms most of his life, but now things were different. Now her father was the boss. That day her parents had stayed at home because the irrigation system on the farm needed fixing.

She knew it wouldn't last forever. Sylvia's family had leased the asparagus farm from a Japanese family, who would someday return.

"The school is right up here," Aunt Soledad announced, jolting Sylvia back into the present. They had entered downtown Westminster: a dozen or so small businesses clustered along a couple of main streets. No churches, no movie theaters, no department stores. It was utterly different from busy Santa Ana, where Sylvia had lived before.

The car turned onto Seventeenth Street, and they passed a large cream-colored stucco building with fancy arches over the doorways and pretty flowerbeds in front. The word *auditorium* was spelled out along the side. She imagined going to assemblies or watching the older kids play sports.

Wow, Sylvia thought.

Her aunt slowed the car and pulled into the parking lot.

"Is that it?" Sylvia whispered to her cousin Virginia. "*That's* our new school?"

"I guess so," Virginia whispered back.

Sylvia had never seen a school like it. Cypress trees and other evergreens surrounded the buildings like tall guards, reminding her of a park and making the place look important.

"Look!" Sylvia cried, pointing at the playground. "Real monkey bars!"

Her old school in Santa Ana didn't have any playground equipment—not even a rope swing on a tree limb. She pictured herself climbing up the ladder and swinging from rung to rung, her legs dangling free beneath her.

"I'm gonna go all the way across without dropping," said Sylvia's younger brother Jerome.

"I'm gonna go all the way across and back again," boasted her other younger brother, Gonzalo junior.

"Come on," Aunt Soledad urged. "There will be time for that later."

Sylvia and the boys followed Aunt Soledad and their two cousins into the front office.

Inside, the school secretary sat behind her desk, pecking away at a typewriter. Sylvia watched, fascinated, as the woman's long, pale fingers tap-danced over the typewriter keys, clickety-clacking out words with a steady beat.

A fan perched on a table across the room swept back and forth, stirring the woman's light brown hair with every pass. She continued typing without even glancing at the newcomers.

"How may I help you?"

"I am Soledad Vidaurri," said Sylvia's aunt, "and I would like to register these children for school."

The secretary fished the enrollment papers out of a desk drawer and handed them to Aunt Soledad. She went back to her typing.

While Aunt Soledad filled out the forms, Sylvia peered out the office door and down the long hallway, its polished floors shining like the surface of a still pond. Across the hall, there was a table with a big stack of brand-new textbooks. Sylvia stepped out, picked up one of the books, and read the title: *Down the Road.* It had a bright yellow cover showing a mother duck followed by five little ducklings.

Sylvia had never held a new textbook before. She closed her eyes and imagined gently opening a book for the very first time, smelling the newness, running her palm over each smooth page, and turning the crisp corners with the tips of her fingers. What would it be like to be the first one to read that book, a book that wasn't worn and soiled by countless other fingers?

Reluctantly she set down the textbook and returned to the office just as Aunt Soledad completed the first set of papers.

"Excuse me, ma'am," Aunt Soledad said to the secretary. "May I have several more forms? For my brother's children?"

The woman stopped typing again. She looked at Sylvia and her brothers as if noticing them for the first time. "Are these your children?"

"No," Aunt Soledad said. "These two are mine." She rested one hand on Alice's shoulder and the other on Virginia's. "They'll be entering third and fourth grade." Sylvia looked at her cousins. They had fair skin and wore their long wavy brown hair in tight curls tied back from their faces with navy ribbons.

"These are my brother's children," Aunt Soledad said, gesturing at Sylvia and her brothers, all three alike with warm brown skin, dark hair, and dark eyes. Jerome and Gonzalo had broad, friendly smiles and neatly combed hair. Sylvia wore her hair in two straight braids, with a red bow pinned above her right ear. She tried to smile, too, but something in the way the woman was looking at them made her uneasy.

"What are their names?" the secretary asked with a sigh.

"Mendez: Sylvia, Gonzalo junior, and Jerome."

The woman held up her hand to interrupt Sylvia's aunt. "The Mendez children will need to register at Hoover School, the Mexican school."

"What? No," Aunt Soledad objected. "I want all of the children in the same school. Both families live in Westminster."

"Mexican children go to the Mexican school," the woman insisted.

"But we live *here*," Aunt Soledad repeated. "All of us. Together." Sylvia and her family lived in the main house on the farm, while Aunt Soledad and her family lived in one of the smaller caretakers' houses.

"I'm sorry, but there is nothing I can do about the rules," the woman said, noisily shutting the desk drawer.

"No, you see, the children are cousins," Aunt Soledad tried again. Her voice remained calm, though Sylvia could see an angry tightening at the corners of her mouth.

"The Mendez children will need to go to the Mexican school."

"But—"

"I can't do anything about it," the secretary said impatiently. "Do you want to register your two or not?"

Sylvia watched her aunt. *Will she listen to the secretary and send us to a different school?*

Aunt Soledad drew in a breath, long and deep, but then she paused and let her breath escape with a sigh.

"No," Aunt Soledad said firmly. "No, I do not want to register my girls."

Sylvia had expected her aunt to let out a furious rush of angry words, but now she realized that those few words were just enough.

Aunt Soledad had nothing more to say. She simply turned around and marched through the open doorway. Sylvia and the other children followed behind her in single file. *We're like the ducklings on the cover of those new textbooks,* Sylvia realized, *the ones that I won't ever get a chance to read.*

On the way home, Aunt Soledad didn't speak. She clutched the steering wheel fiercely and glared at the road.

Virginia and Gonzalo rode in the front seat, and Sylvia was squeezed between Jerome and Alice in the back, their forearms touching. Sylvia looked down at her hands, her skin the color of dark caramel, and then she looked at Alice's hands, which reminded her more of *dulce de leche,* "milk candy"—lighter, creamier, paler than her own.

Is this why they would take Alice and Virginia but not me? she wondered. *Is it because my skin is too brown? Is this why me and my brothers were told to go to the Mexican school? But I'm not even Mexican. I'm American.*

What is my father going to say about this?

Sylvia gazed out the window. It was so unfair to everyone. Her mother was an American citizen from Puerto Rico. Her father had come from Mexico as a little boy, but he had become a United States citizen and worked hard all his life.

How many times had her father told her that he wanted her to get the best education possible, to be the first in the family to finish high school, to go to college? She could hear his voice: "I want you to have every opportunity I never had." Her father would be so disappointed if she didn't go to Westminster School.

Maybe Hoover School will be just as good as Westminster School. Maybe going to Westminster School doesn't really matter. Maybe my father won't be disappointed.

But she couldn't help thinking about the monkey bars and the new textbooks, and her heart sank. She guessed there would be no monkey bars and no new textbooks at Hoover School. It would be like her old school in Santa Ana: secondhand, second-best.

We're being treated like second-best people, she thought bitterly.

A few minutes later they turned off the main road and onto the long driveway with asparagus fields on either side. The farm buildings consisted of the main house, a bunkhouse and three other smaller houses behind it, and a large barn with an open packing house beside it.

Aunt Soledad made a dramatic entrance: she braked hard and fast, bringing the Pontiac to a sudden stop. She yanked the key out of the ignition, slammed the car door, and stormed off toward the packing house.

"Gonzalo!" she called, looking for her brother. "Gonzalo!"

Sylvia and the others trailed Aunt Soledad. The afternoon sun fell in dusty streaks, highlighting crates of freshly picked asparagus. The air smelled of rich, wet soil. A couple of brown and white hens wandered past, pecking at the ground in sudden jerks.

Sylvia's father looked up from his conversation with several packers. "What's the matter?" he asked his sister.

"The kids, they can't go to that school," Aunt Soledad said in a rush. "The secretary said that the kids have to go to Hoover School because they're Mexican."

Aunt Soledad didn't mention right away that Alice and Virginia could have enrolled at Westminster. *Maybe she's trying not to embarrass our family,* Sylvia thought.

"That can't be right," he said. "Westminster's the closest school."

"I know," Aunt Soledad said. "But they're supposed to go to that school for Mexican children."

To Sylvia's surprise, her father didn't seem upset. He smiled and rested his hand on Aunt Soledad's shoulder. "Don't worry. There must be a mistake. I'll take care of it tomorrow."

Sylvia relaxed. She had every faith that her father would be able to set things right.

Later that afternoon, Sylvia went to her room to put away the navy jumper and new school shoes her mother had bought her.

"Sylvia?" Her mother pushed open the bedroom door with a dish towel in one hand, taking a break from fixing dinner for the farm workers. "Your father told me what happened when you went to register for school." She studied Sylvia's face carefully.

"Yeah, Aunt Soledad was pretty angry," said Sylvia.

"I am, too."

"Mom," Sylvia began, "do you think we'll be able to go to Westminster School?"

"I don't see why not," Sylvia's mother answered. "That's the closest school."

"But the lady at the school said we have to go to a separate school for Mexicans, next to the barrio."

"So?" said her mother. "We don't live in the barrio."

"I know."

"Your father will handle it."

The oven timer sounded in the kitchen. "The cornbread is ready," Sylvia's mother said. "Do you want your door open or closed?"

"Open is fine."

"Don't worry so much. It will all work out. You'll see." Then her mother left.

Sylvia turned back to her closet. She picked up the box her new shoes had come in and pushed it onto the high shelf in her closet. Instead of sliding in completely, the box stopped three-quarters of the way back. She shoved harder, but it was blocked by something at the back of the shelf, something she couldn't see.

Sylvia dragged the ladder-back chair from her desk over to the closet and climbed onto it. She reached up, moved the shoe box aside, and stretched out her hand, running it back and forth over the shelf. She felt something but accidentally nudged it just beyond her grasp.

She stood on her tiptoes and stretched again. This time she was able to grab the corner of a poster or paper of some kind. She dragged the paper—and whatever was resting on top of it—to the edge of the shelf. A sprinkling of dust showered down on her.

"Ugh!" Sylvia cried, wiping her face with her arm. She reached up again and pulled down her treasure: a delicate Japanese doll and a photograph.

Sylvia stepped down and set the photograph on her bed. She shook the dust from the doll and blew it away as well as she could. The doll had black hair, blunt-cut at the shoulders with straight bangs across her forehead. She wore a shimmering red satin robe made of fabric as nice as that in her mother's best dress.

Why would someone leave a doll like this behind? Sylvia wondered. *Did someone forget it? Did someone leave it here for me to play with?*

"Your name is Keiko," Sylvia told the doll. She didn't have any Japanese friends, but she had heard the name before.

Sylvia placed Keiko on her pillow, next to the Mexican doll her mother had given her. Carmencita wore a three-tiered skirt made of pink, turquoise, and purple cotton, edged with zigzag trim in green and yellow.

"Carmencita, meet Keiko," Sylvia said. "Keiko, this is Carmencita." She leaned the two dolls against her pillow.

Then Sylvia reached for the black-and-white photograph. Three rows of children and a young woman—surely their teacher—smiled at the camera. Two girls in the front row held a sign: WESTMINSTER SCHOOL, 3RD GRADE, MRS. HOWARD, 1941–1942.

Turning the photo over, Sylvia read the name "Aki Munemitsu" written on the back in shaky cursive.

Sylvia peered more closely at the photograph and spotted a girl with almond eyes in the second row. Right away, she guessed: *This was Aki's photograph; this was Aki's bedroom. So Keiko must have been Aki's doll, before she had to go away.*

Sylvia knew the Japanese family had been sent away because of the war, which was how her family had been able to lease the farm. After the United States had entered the war against Japan and Germany, all the Japanese along the coast of California had to leave their homes and move to inland camps until the war was over.

How sad for them, Sylvia thought. *But how lucky for us that we get to live here, even for a little while.*

Sylvia put the photograph down and looked out the bedroom window at row after row of lacy asparagus plants. The late afternoon sun hung low in the sky, painting gold on everything it touched. The farm looked so pretty at that moment. Still, Sylvia could not let go of two important questions.

Where is Aki now?

And if a Japanese girl like Aki was allowed to go to Westminster School, why can't I?

CHAPTER 2

Fall seven times; stand up eight.
—JAPANESE PROVERB

Aki
Westminster, California, eight months earlier

Aki Munemitsu expected to finish third grade at Westminster School. She planned to complete her book report on *Call It Courage* by Armstrong Sperry and present her oral report. She imagined she would attend the end-of-the-year picnic and jump rope with the other girls in Mrs. Howard's class. And she thought that when she came home on the last day of third grade her father would be there to say, "Happy summer!" and take her out for ice cream.

Aki never expected the one thing that actually happened: she was forced to leave behind her home, her school, her father—her whole life.

The trouble started on a Sunday afternoon. It was December 7, 1941. Aki sat at the dining room table with her math homework spread out before her. It was problems in long division: two-digit divisors into four-digit dividends, with remainders. From time to time Aki repeated her teacher's instructions: "Find the quotient; check your work." In the kitchen, her mother cleaned up the lunch dishes while the radio played a piano sonata. Aki's head was filled with numbers and music.

And then the music stopped.

"We interrupt this program to bring you a special news bulletin," said a man's deep, serious voice. "The Japanese have attacked Pearl Harbor, Hawaii, by air."

Aki laid down her pencil and joined her mother, who was standing by the sink with her right hand over her mouth. They both stared at the radio, listening closely to every word. Together they learned that at 7:53 A.M. Hawaii time, Japanese airplanes had bombed the United States naval station at Pearl Harbor. No one knew how many Americans were dead or how many ships had been destroyed.

When the report ended, Aki asked, "What does this mean?"

"War," her mother said. "It means there will be war."

The word *war* and her mother's worried tone made Aki's stomach tighten. *But why should we be worried?* she asked herself. *Hawaii is far away from California. What does a war being fought in places I've never heard of have to do with us?*

When Aki's father and older brother came in from the fields, they received the news in bewildered silence. Aki wondered, since both of her parents had been born in Japan, if they were ashamed of what their home country had done. And were they afraid of what their new country, the United States, was going to do?

Overnight, Aki's world changed.

She watched neighbors turn against their neighbors: people refused to shop in Japanese-owned stores or hire Japanese employees.

Whispers and suspicious looks often followed her and her family on their visits into town. She heard strangers mutter under their breath as they passed by: "Go back to where you came from."

Aki and her family suddenly had the face of the enemy. They were loyal Americans, but many people assumed that anyone of Japanese ancestry would support Japan rather than the United States in the war.

Community-wide blackouts were enforced. Anxious families turned off their lights or hung blankets in front of their windows so that their homes wouldn't be easy targets for nighttime bombers should the enemy ever make its way to California. Aki sometimes felt she lived in darkness: hiding any light, listening for the roar of enemy planes or the *boom boom boom* of falling bombs. Night brought the war close. And it was too easy, in the dark, to imagine neighbors agreeing that it was people like the Munemitsus who had brought things to this terrible point.

A few days after President Roosevelt declared war on Japan, Aki saw a man standing on the street in Westminster with a sign: I AM CHINESE, NOT JAPANESE.

For the first time in her life, Aki wondered if there was something wrong with being Japanese. And if that were true, then there was something wrong with *her*. She began to think of being Japanese as not merely different but *bad*.

❧

A few months later, Aki and her mother went into downtown Westminster to shop for groceries. They noticed that posters had been placed on storefront windows and bulletin boards all over town.

They read the one posted at the entrance to the library. It began INSTRUCTIONS TO ALL PERSONS OF JAPA-

NESE ANCESTRY and went on to declare that everyone with Japanese ancestors—even people who had only a single great-great-grandparent who was Japanese—had to register with the Civil Control Station for evacuation.

"What is evacuation?" Aki asked her mother.

"It means leaving, moving someplace else."

"Where?"

"I don't know." Her mother's voice sounded flat and tired.

"Do we have to go?"

"Yes, this says we will all have to go."

"How long will we be gone?"

"I don't know," her mother repeated.

A few days later, Aki's father went to Santa Ana to register the family with the government. When he returned he sank into an oversized chair in the living room.

"Come here," he said, patting his lap. "Sit with me."

Aki stepped toward him, but she stopped short of sitting. When she was younger Aki used to climb her father like a mountain, scaling his legs and exploring the forest of whiskers on his cheeks. But that was a long time ago.

Doesn't he understand that I'm no longer a child?

He reached out for her, but Aki didn't take his hands.

"I'm not a baby," she said.

"Of course not," her father replied with a small smile. "You're right. Now, there is much to do."

Her father explained that they had only a few days to sell or secure all of their belongings. Each family member was allowed to pack a single suitcase or box with sheets, towels, dishes, and a limited amount of clothing.

"That's all," Aki's father said. "We can only bring what we can carry."

There was no time to waste. Later that afternoon, Aki's father and her brother went to the First Western Bank in Garden Grove for a meeting with Mr. Monroe, the banker, about the farm. Aki wanted to go with her father, but she knew it was Seiko who helped to translate between English and Japanese when her father conducted business.

Aki found her mother sitting alone at the dining room table. She didn't smile when Aki came into the room. No one smiled very much anymore.

Without speaking, Aki sat across from her mother. The table was stacked with many of their family's most prized possessions. While Aki watched, her mother picked up a small white ceramic bowl decorated with hand-painted red poppies.

"This belonged to your grandmother, my mother, back in Japan," Aki's mother whispered.

Aki watched, her throat dry, as her mother carefully wrapped the bowl in brown paper and nestled it into the little wooden chest in front of her.

"I carried it in this chest when I came here."

Aki's mother reached for a rectangular tray of black lacquer with a delicate painting of a bird and a signature in Japanese characters in one corner. She tried to fit it into the wooden box, but it was too big. She sighed and said, "This one is not so important. It's not from our family." She set it aside.

"What are you going to do with it?" Aki asked.

"We must pack up or get rid of everything from Japan," her mother said. "If we keep too many things from Japan, people may think we love Japan more than we love the United States."

"But that isn't true," Aki protested.

"There is so much mistrust, so much anger everywhere. I couldn't bear to think of these things in the hands of people who would find them ugly and hateful." Aki's mother shook her head sadly. "We can put some things in the attic, but we cannot be sure they will be there when we return."

The war will be over someday, Aki thought, *but so many of our beautiful things may be gone forever.* Aki kept this thought to herself. In a world where so little made sense to her anymore, Aki would simply trust her mother and father and their decisions.

Aki watched her mother pack, hoping that just sitting there, quietly being with her, helped her mother feel less alone. And that was all Aki could do.

When the table was cleared and the non-Japanese dishes and serving pieces were returned to the china cabinet, Aki's mother said, "We have more to do." She went to the hall closet and pulled from a shelf an old shoe box filled with family photographs.

Aki recognized the envelope of photos that her father had carried with him when he moved from Kochi-ken, Japan, to the United States in 1915. She knew he had come to America alone when he was just sixteen years old. He had been eager to work on a farm where the land was plentiful and more fertile than in his ancestral home on the Japanese island of Shikoku, the smallest of the four main islands that made up the Japanese homeland. Aki's mother also came from Kochi-ken, but she had come to the United States later.

Her mother opened a box and picked up a photograph of a young man wearing a wide-brimmed straw hat and standing in an asparagus field. "This was your father not long after we married," Aki's mother said, holding the photograph so that Aki could see it. Aki recalled the story of how her father returned to Japan to find a wife. After her parents married, they moved to southern California and worked as farmers.

"He has always been such a hardworking man," Aki's mother said. Then she set the photograph aside.

Aki's mother reached for another photograph. Her fingers trembled when she picked up an image of a young woman holding an infant. Aki loved this picture of her mother, so young and proud and hopeful.

"Your brother was such a lovely baby," Aki's mother whispered. Aki looked at her mother and then at the picture, and she, too, forgot for a moment what they were doing and felt her mother's affection for them all.

"Tell me again the story of Seiko's name," Aki asked gently.

"We have a lot of work to do," her mother said briskly, but she could not stop herself from remembering. She started the story the way she always did: "Your brother was born on February thirteenth, 1922."

"And you didn't know what to name him," Aki eagerly volunteered. She felt the two were like actors, going over the familiar lines of a deeply loved script.

"That's right," her mother said.

"You went into labor on President Lincoln's birthday," Aki said.

"Yes. The pains started on February twelfth, and your brother was born on the following morning," Aki's mother said. "Your father and I wanted to honor our Japanese heritage, but we also knew that we were Americans now. So we named our baby Seiko Lincoln—Seiko for your grandfather and our Japanese ancestry and Lincoln in honor of the sixteenth president of the United States."

"It's a good thing he wasn't born on the fourteenth," Aki said, setting up the punch line.

"That's right. Or we might have named him Seiko Valentine."

They laughed, and Aki felt a little better. The story belonged to her family. It was a part of her that could never be taken away. It felt good knowing that it would remain safe in their hearts, not left behind like old photographs or pottery.

Aki's mother set Seiko's baby picture aside.

One by one, Aki and her mother looked at dozens of pictures. Then Aki's mother gathered a small pile of photographs, which she tucked into an envelope and slipped into the wooden chest. Aki studied each of the remaining photos, trying to memorize the images before they were lost. When she was finished, she handed the photographs back to her mother, who tore each one in half and then dropped the pieces into a wastebasket.

~

As the time drew closer for them to leave, Aki thought more and more about the unfairness of having to leave behind her farm, her school, and her friends. She recalled her mother's response the first time she'd asked, "Why do we have to be evacuated?"

"It's complicated," her mother had explained. "Some people believe that people from Japan are a threat to our national security."

"How am I a threat to national security?" Aki had asked.

"You're not," her mother had reassured her. "But the government doesn't know that. We'll just cooperate so that we can be home as soon as possible."

As Aki helped her mother pack, the wrongness of it all swept over her.

"Do we have to sell everything we don't take with us?" Aki asked. She had seen other Japanese families selling their cars, refrigerators, bicycles, and other valuables on the side of the road.

"No, no," assured her mother. "We are lucky. Mr. Monroe will help us."

Aki knew that her parents trusted Mr. Monroe, the banker who had helped them buy the farm. Her father wasn't allowed to buy land because he had never become an American citizen. But Mr. Monroe had found a way around this: Aki's brother had been born in the United States and was a citizen, so Mr. Monroe made Seiko the legal owner of the farm.

Aki looked out her bedroom window at row after row of asparagus plants. "Will we have to give up the farm?" she asked.

"I don't think so," her mother said. "Mr. Monroe will find someone who can take care of it while we're gone."

Aki looked around her bedroom. "What about my room? My things?"

"You can take what we can fit into this suitcase."

Aki's suitcase suddenly seemed very small.

One suitcase is not enough, she thought hopelessly.

Her mother began packing sheets, towels, clothing, and toiletries.

My entire world cannot fit into one tiny suitcase, cried the voice in Aki's mind.

She grabbed the rag doll her mother had made for her and tucked it in her suitcase between a nightgown and a sweater.

Her mother closed the suitcase, reached into her apron pocket, and pulled out a manila cardstock tag with a long string. On the card someone had written the family name, Munemitsu, and the word *Poston*. The card was stamped with five red numbers: 13527. She tied one tag to the bag and placed a duplicate on the top of Aki's dresser.

"One tag stays on the luggage," Aki's mother said. "And one is for you to keep."

Aki looked around her room at the clothes and toys that did not fit in the suitcase.

"Someday all these things can be replaced," her mother said, following her gaze. Then she stopped and corrected herself: "Most of these things can be replaced."

On the bed, next to the suitcase, Aki had placed her favorite doll, a dancer with a porcelain face and red-painted lips, the one with a red silk kimono and real hair cut into bangs. Her father had given her the doll when she was a tiny baby. It was the only thing she had that came from him alone.

Without her mother saying anything, Aki knew that she could not keep the doll. It was Japanese. *Bad.*

"We will try to find another one when the time is right," her mother said. She picked up the doll and started to leave. Aki knew the doll was headed for the wastebasket.

Aki had done her best to be strong for her mother, but she couldn't stop her eyes from filling with tears. She tried to distract herself by counting the number of wooden boards across the floor.

One . . . two . . . three . . .

"I'm so, so sorry," her mother whispered, handing her daughter the doll. "Put it where it will be safe."

Aki took the little dancer, then slipped her arms around her mother's waist. They clung to each other for a long time. When Aki finally eased her grip, her mother watched while Aki dragged a chair over to the closet and stretched in order to place the doll at the back of the top shelf, where it was hidden from view. Somewhere on that shelf she had already placed her class photo from Westminster School. Hers was only one small face in a crowd of classmates; surely it wouldn't offend anyone who might find it. Aki hoped that her hidden treasures—the doll and the photograph, both part of a happier time—would be waiting for her whenever she came back.

CHAPTER 3

He who labors and thrives spins gold.
—MEXICAN PROVERB

Sylvia
Westminster, California

Sylvia studied Keiko carefully. The doll was about six inches tall and had tiny, delicate porcelain hands. Sylvia rested one of Keiko's hands against the tip of her finger. The doll's fingers were long and thin and white, posed in a relaxed and graceful position with the thumbs slightly extended away from the other fingers.

Her hands look real, Sylvia thought.

Sylvia held out her hand and tried to imitate Keiko's pose. It didn't look right: her own hand seemed so clumsy when she compared it to the delicate dancer's. Sylvia began to examine her hands as if she had never seen them before, inspecting the lines that ran across her palms as well as the intricate, fine swirls of her fingerprints. Her hands belonged to her and no one else; no two like them existed anywhere on earth. Yet others used their own hands to hold her and her brothers back and even wave them away.

She wiggled her fingers, imagining them darting at a typewriter like the secretary's at Westminster School. She used both hands to pretend that she was dicing vegetables on a chopping block: *chop chop chop*. She thought about her mother's strong brown hands, so skilled, so fast at slicing onions or braiding hair. She could never think of her mother's busy hands being as still as Keiko's.

Then she thought of her father's powerful hands— they were never idle, either. In the fields, his hands constantly moved, tirelessly reaching and snipping fruit from the trees or slashing asparagus stalks in a single swift motion. Sylvia imitated the motion of her father's hands, flashing back and forth from fruit to burlap bag.

His strong hands had a story to tell. Whenever Sylvia's father came in from the fields, he scrupulously scrubbed his hands and neatly trimmed fingernails, making them as clean as a businessman's. But his hands could not keep secrets: he couldn't soften the thick, leathery calluses that identified him as a man used to hard physical work.

Knock! Knock! Knock!

Sylvia jumped. She hadn't heard her brothers come to her bedroom door.

Seven-year-old Gonzalo junior peeked inside. Jerome, two years younger, slipped in behind him.

"Mom wants you to come with us," Gonzalo said. "Dad's home."

Sylvia put Keiko on her bedside table, carefully leaning her against the lamp. "See you later," Sylvia promised before following her brothers to the dining room. Her parents were already sitting at the table talking.

Her father wore pleated brown slacks and a freshly ironed collared white shirt. His tie was loosened around his neck and his suit coat hung on the back of the chair.

Sylvia knew that earlier their father had gone to talk to someone about getting them into Westminster School. Although she was eager to find out what had happened, she knew her father would tell them in his own time.

Jerome was not as patient.

"What did the man say?" he asked. "Do we get to go to Westminster?" School started in just a few days.

Sylvia's father turned toward him. "That's what your mother and I are talking about. The man I had an appointment with this morning is Richard Harris, the superintendent of schools in Westminster. I told Mr. Harris that we do not live in the barrio." Westminster's barrio was the poor neighborhood near Olive Street—and Hoover School. "I told him that we live on the Munemitsu farm on the other side of town."

"And closer to Westminster School," Sylvia's mother added.

"Yes," her father agreed, "closer to Westminster School."

He paused.

Everyone waited, the silence slowing time.

"But Superintendent Harris said we still need to register at Hoover School," Sylvia's father said with a shrug of his shoulders.

Sylvia's stomach flip-flopped. This was not the news she had expected.

"That's not fair!" she blurted out.

"The children belong at Westminster School," her mother declared.

"I know, I know," her father said, holding up his hands in mock surrender. "Mr. Harris said, 'The problem is that if we admit your children, then other parents will want their children to go to Westminster, too.'"

"And what's wrong with that?" Sylvia's mother demanded.

"Nothing," her husband replied. "Of course, nothing. We all want what is best for our children."

Sylvia's father looked down at his hands and inspected his fingernails. He swiped the thumbnail of his right hand under the perfect white crescents of the nails on his left hand. It was a nervous habit; Sylvia could see that his fingernails were as clean as ever.

"Mr. Harris told me he knew that times were changing," Sylvia's father said. "He said that he would talk to some people at the board of education and see if anything could be done."

"So what are we going to do now?" Sylvia's mother asked.

"We will enroll the children at Hoover School." Her father's voice was decisive. "But this is not the end."

⤛

Several days later, on the first day of school, Sylvia woke up before her alarm clock rang. She stared at the ceiling, anxious about the day ahead. *Will I like my teacher?* she wondered. *Will I make friends in my new class? Even if Hoover School isn't as fancy as*

Westminster School, it surely will be nicer than my last school.

As the sun finally peeked over the mountains, Sylvia put on her first-day outfit: a navy jumper and short-sleeved white cotton shirt with a Peter Pan collar. She wore her new school shoes and carried a brand-new three-ring binder filled with ruled paper. Inside a small pouch she had five yellow pencils as well as two bubblegum-pink erasers, which were still perfect, no gray smudges.

When Sylvia stepped out of her bedroom, she heard her mother singing. Her mother was like a radio that switched on in the morning and turned off late at night. Singing and humming were as natural to her as the rhythm of her own heartbeat. Even over the past few days, when the family had been worried about the start of the school year, she had kept singing. Today Sylvia recognized her mother's favorite song, *"Cielito Lindo"*—"Pretty Sweetheart."

> *Ay, ay, ay, ay*
> *Canta y no llores,*
> *Porque cantando se alegran,*
> *Cielito lindo, los corazones.*

Ay, ay, ay, ay
Sing a tune and don't cry,
Because, through singing, my dear,
We can bring cheer to our hearts.

~~~

That morning Sylvia's mother sang while she was fixing breakfast. She sang while weaving Sylvia's hair into two long braids, and while tying navy blue ribbons in Sylvia's hair.

But her mother's singing couldn't hide the fact that today was a day of disappointment. Sylvia was getting ready to go to a school that was a bitter letdown to her parents and herself. It was only her little brothers who didn't seem to give the matter much thought. One school was the same as another to them; as long as there was recess and not too much homework, they would be content.

At first Sylvia had thought Virginia and Alice would be with her on the first day, but right after the incident at Westminster School, their father got a job as a foreman at a farm about thirty miles away and they had moved. Sylvia and her brothers were left to face Hoover School alone.

"Okay, okay," her mother said when it was finally time to leave. "*Bésame,*" she ordered with a smile. "Kiss me."

Sylvia kissed her mother on the cheek, then walked with her brothers on the hard-packed earth edging the fields to the main road, where the school bus would pick them up. Jerome kicked a rock and followed it from point to point, staying more or less on the path.

In the distance Sylvia saw two girls already waiting for the bus. One of them looked close to her age, the other a bit younger.

Those girls probably go to Westminster, she thought.

Holding her notebook against her chest, Sylvia walked right up to the older girl.

"Hello," she said, offering a small smile and a slight nod, hoping her nervousness didn't show. Then she asked, "Is this where we catch the school bus?"

"Hi," the older girl said. She had shoulder-length honey-colored hair pulled back in a ponytail. "Don't worry. You're in the right place, and just in time."

Just then a golden yellow school bus chugged up the road and groaned to a halt in front of the waiting group.

Sylvia stood back, allowing the other kids to board first. She wanted to see where everyone else sat before choosing a place of her own.

She scanned the unfamiliar faces on the bus. Everyone was white. *Everyone.*

Sylvia paused next to the seat where the girl who'd spoken to her was sitting, but then she moved on, afraid the girl might be saving the space for someone else. As the bus lurched into motion, she headed unsteadily to the back and sat on a seat across from her brothers.

She murmured to Gonzalo, "Are we on the wrong bus?"

Her brother grinned. "Don't you think the driver would have said something?"

"Maybe there's a separate bus for kids going to Hoover School."

But Gonzalo wasn't interested in her concerns. He turned to whisper something to Jerome, and the two boys burst out laughing.

Although Sylvia knew that most Mexicans lived in the barrio on the other side of Westminster, she hadn't dreamed that she and her brothers would be the only brown-skinned passengers on the bus.

Several stops later, the bus pulled up in front of Westminster School. She looked longingly at the lovely buildings and the fully equipped playground.

"Stay here," Sylvia told her brothers, who had started to get up and follow the other children.

The three of them sat in their seats while everyone else stepped off and headed toward the entrance.

"What are you all waiting for?" the bus driver asked impatiently, looking at Sylvia and her brothers in the rearview mirror. He wore sunglasses that hid any expression.

"This isn't our school," Sylvia responded, her voice higher than usual. "We go to Hoover School."

"Yeah," he said, "I know." Now he sounded bored. He had slipped off his sunglasses and was polishing them with the corner of a handkerchief.

Sylvia didn't know what to do. She looked at her brothers, who looked back uncertainly.

"You walk the rest of the way," the driver said.

"Oh. Thank you," she said. "We didn't know."

Clutching her binder, Sylvia exited the bus, followed by Gonzalo and Jerome. She looked up and down the street, searching for a clue that would tell her which way to go.

"We don't know the way," she called back to the driver, as he was reaching for the lever that would close the bus door.

"Go on down to Olive Street and turn right," the man said, pointing. "Hoover School is at Olive and Maple. You can't miss it." The door closed, and the bus pulled away from the curb.

The school is right next to the barrio, Sylvia thought, her heart sinking even lower.

She and her brothers walked together, lost in their own thoughts.

The first day of third grade isn't starting out the way I hoped, Sylvia admitted to herself. Gonzalo kept his head down and his hands shoved deep in his pants pockets. Even Jerome couldn't seem to find the energy to kick a rock.

After about ten minutes of trudging along, Gonzalo said, "There it is."

Further along the street was a run-down, dirty clapboard building next to a cow pasture. Loose dirt and clumps of weeds surrounded the school. An empty field stood in for a playground, sure to be dusty in warm weather, a sea of mud when it rained. No guardian trees and thick green lawns here. A faded, hand-painted sign posted above the building's front door read HOOVER SCHOOL. The smell of cow manure filled Sylvia's nose.

This place was going to be just like all the other Mexican schools she and her brothers had attended— nothing but out-of-date hand-me-down textbooks with pages torn or missing and secondhand desks scarred with pencil marks and initials.

Once again, we get the leftovers.

When Sylvia's class broke for lunch, there were already several other groups outside on the back field. Sylvia sat under a shade tree with Ramona, a girl from her class who lived in the barrio.

"Shoo!" Sylvia cried, swishing at a swarm of flies. "Leave me alone!" A fly landed on her bologna sandwich as she took a bite.

"They come from the cow pasture. You'll get used to it," Ramona said. "They never go away."

"I'll never get used to it," Sylvia said.

"What other choice is there?"

Westminster School, she wanted to answer. But it wasn't a choice. At least not for her and Ramona. Instead she just shrugged, waved off another fly, and took a second bite of her sandwich.

As she was finishing, she noticed a younger boy approach the wire fence that surrounded the pasture, keeping the cows inside and the children out. One wire strung along the top of the fence glinted wickedly in the sunlight. The boy was tentatively reaching his hand toward that wire.

"Aaaagh!" the boy cried, loud enough to silence the yard, at least for a moment.

The boy pulled his hand back and shook it violently.

Some of the older boys laughed.

"It's electric," said Ramona. "Someone probably dared him to touch it. He's in second grade; this is his first year at Hoover. It always happens to a new kid on the first day of school."

Sylvia rubbed her hands together, imagining the jolt of electricity that must have passed through the boy's hand.

Who would put an electric fence next to a school?

At the end of the day, Sylvia walked with her brothers back to Westminster School. When they arrived, the other kids were already boarding the bus. Sylvia slipped into a vacant seat in the middle of the bus; again, Gonzalo and Jerome sat across the aisle.

On the ride home Sylvia thought about that second-grader. She remembered his cry, and then his pain, embarrassment, and shame.

She leaned over and whispered to Jerome and Gonzalo: "Tomorrow, at school, whatever you do, don't touch the fence."

From the looks on her brothers' faces she could tell that they already knew.

Sylvia looked out the window as they passed one farm after another, each separated from its neighbor by a fence. Split-rail fences, electric fences, barbed-wire fences—keeping some in, shutting others out. Sylvia replayed the moment when she'd seen the boy get shocked. She, too, had once been shocked while plugging in a lamp, so she knew the burning jolt he must have felt.

Her mind wandered to her father and his efforts to break down the barrier that kept her from Westminster School, from a good education. *He's not going to back down,* Sylvia thought. *But I sure hope he doesn't get burned.*

CHAPTER 4

If you stand up like a nail,
you will get hammered down.
—JAPANESE PROVERB

Aki
Westminster and Santa Ana, California

The day after Aki hid her doll and began her final packing, she came home from school to find her mother standing at the sink, slicing cabbage for *korokke*—Japanese croquettes. Aki dropped her book bag on the dining room table and went into the kitchen to get a glass of water.

Her mother didn't look up. She didn't say "Welcome home" or "How was your day?" She stood silently, chopping and rechopping the greens. For a moment there was only the faint crunch of cabbage leaves on the cutting board. When she stopped, Aki saw her mother wipe her cheek with the back of her hand.

"What is it?" Aki asked.

"It's Pop," her mother said, her voice breaking. She cleared her throat and started again. "He's been taken to a camp." She spoke in a whisper, so sad and so faint that Aki could hardly hear.

"What?"

"He was taken to a camp," her mother repeated.

"When?"

"Several men came for him this morning, after you left for school."

As if from very far off, Aki heard the rush of the water pouring into the sink and smelled the open bottle of sesame oil on the counter. The loose hair at the nape of her mother's neck, the blade of the knife in the white sink, the texture of her mother's dress—the light blue one with white piping at the collar—all came into focus, sharp focus, like a snapshot of this moment that she would never be able to forget.

Aki didn't know how long she hesitated before saying, "I thought we were going to be together."

"I did, too." Her mother wiped her cheek again. "And we will be."

"When?" Aki repeated.

"I don't know. I don't know exactly when, but he will be back." Her mother's voice grew stronger as she spoke.

Now tears flowed down Aki's face, and she let them. Her mother pulled her close. Aki put her arms around her mother's tiny waist and they leaned into each other, holding each other up.

She whispered: "I didn't get to say good-bye." The realization struck her like a slap: her father was gone, and she hadn't been able to hug him or to tell him, "I love you."

"No good-byes," her mother said, her voice firm now. "No *sayonaras*."

At that moment, Aki could imagine what her father would say if he were there. He would pat her on the shoulder and say, "Be strong." She could find strength in that.

Did I see him in the kitchen this morning? What were his last words to me?

She wanted a perfect picture of him in her mind to hang on to. But her mind was blank.

"I miss him already," Aki whispered.

"I do, too," her mother said.

Aki and her mother were quiet for a while.

"I still don't understand," Aki finally said. "Why did they come just for Pop?"

"They took some of the men first," her mother said. "Newspaper reporters, teachers, businessmen like Pop—men they thought might be a threat."

"A threat?" Aki echoed. "Pop isn't a threat to anyone. If he is, then why didn't they take all of us? Aren't we all threats?"

"I know, I know," her mother said. "But the people who make the rules don't know. They are scared of anyone who is Japanese."

"Even us?"

"Even us." Aki's mother shook her head.

"What about Seiko?" At age seventeen, Aki's older brother was almost a man. Ever since he was a little boy, he had helped his father run the farm, going with his father to the bank to translate back and forth between Japanese and English.

"He'll be with us at a different camp." Aki welcomed this small bit of good news.

"We will be leaving in a couple of days," Aki's mother added. "For a place called Poston, in Arizona."

Poston, Aki thought. *The word on the luggage tag on that too-small suitcase.*

∾

That night Aki tossed and turned, waking before dawn, feverish and thirsty. She called for her mother, who entered the bedroom and turned on the over-head light. The brightness hurt, and she had to squint until her eyes adjusted to the glare.

Her mother's eyes were swollen and red. Aki wondered whether her mother had slept at all, or if she had spent the night crying.

"Are you sick?" Aki's mother asked. "Let me look at you." She felt Aki's face and neck, and then lifted her nightgown.

"Oh, no," her mother said. Aki's legs and torso were covered with tiny red spots, as if she had been attacked by a swarm of hungry mosquitoes. "Chicken pox."

"Why *now*?" Aki had hoped to get chicken pox the year before, when several of her friends came down with it and got to stay home from school for a couple of weeks. Aki didn't want to be sick now. She didn't want to give her mother anything more to worry about.

"What will happen to me?" Aki asked.

"You must not scratch," her mother said. "Let me get a thermometer and a lotion for the itching. You can have an oatmeal bath in the morning."

But Aki couldn't help asking again, "What's going to happen to me?"

"You'll be fine in a week or two," her mother said.

"No, what's going to happen to me when you leave for the camp?"

Aki's mother stared at her a moment. Her face sagged. "I don't know," she said. "I'll find out what to do about that in the morning."

Aki tried not to scratch. *At least we have something new to think about, instead of Pop and packing and Poston.*

Aki heard her mother rummaging in the bathroom medicine cabinet. She returned with calamine lotion and dabbed it on the reddest spots. Soon the itching stopped long enough for Aki to fall asleep.

When Aki finally awoke in the morning, her mother was leaning over her.

"How are you feeling?"

"Itchy," Aki said. "Really itchy."

Aki's mother began to fold the blanket on the end of the bed. "I'm afraid there isn't much time." She looked at Aki and then at the suitcase next to the bed.

"I talked to the man at the Civil Control Station. I asked if we could stay until you were better," she said. "But he said no. We have to go now."

"But I'm sick!"

"You must go to the hospital in Santa Ana, and Seiko and I must go ahead to Poston. They don't want the chicken pox to spread all through the camp."

"I have to go to the hospital? By myself?" Aki knew she sounded like a whining baby, but she couldn't help herself.

First, Pop gone. Now, even more separation. She reached for her mother's hand.

"Don't be afraid," Aki's mother said. "In the hospital, the nurses will bring you food on a tray so that you can eat in your bed!"

Aki knew that her mother was trying to put on a cheerful face for her, and silently she resolved, *I will try to be happy, Mom—for you.* But all she really wanted was to have her father back, to stay on the farm, to go back to school—to have things be the way they'd been before the evacuation.

But what I want doesn't matter.

That afternoon, when the front door clicked shut behind her, Aki knew she was leaving behind everything that was familiar and comfortable. It was as though she were walking away from her life.

⁂

Aki's mother set the suitcase next to the empty bed in the hospital room. Aki looked over at the Japanese girl in the next bed. She could tell by the red splotches on her roommate's face and arms that she had chicken pox, too. The girls greeted each other while Aki's mother unpacked some of the items from the suitcase.

When her mother could find nothing more to do, she said, "Well, I better let you two girls get some rest."

Aki felt her stomach flutter.

Aki's mother put her arms around her and held her close. She didn't say good-bye. "I will see you soon." Then she leaned over and kissed Aki on the top of her head and whispered in her ear: "*Gaman*," the Japanese word for "Be brave, be strong."

Aki looked up at her mother with tears in her eyes. Her mother's eyes were wet, too. *I will not cry, I will not cry,* Aki chanted to herself. *I will not embarrass my mother, not in front of a stranger.*

Aki's mother let go, and Aki felt her mother's warmth fade away.

"Do you want to play checkers?" Aki's new roommate, Yuki, asked before Aki's mother had even left the room.

Aki tried to make her voice sound cheerful. "Okay."

As Yuki began to set up the game on one of the bedside tables, Aki strained to hear the sound of her mother's heels striking the linoleum floor in the hall. She listened long after the footsteps had faded away.

"Which camp are you going to?" Yuki asked.

"Poston."

"Me too!" Yuki divided the checkers into piles of red and black. "My family has already gone."

"What have they told you about it?"

"Nothing," the girl said. She stacked the checkers to make sure the piles were even and all the pieces were there. "I just got here yesterday. My mother says we'll find out when we get there."

"Maybe we'll be neighbors," Aki said.

"I hope so," said Yuki. "Do you want red or black?"

"It doesn't matter."

Yuki turned the board so that the red checkers were on Aki's side. "Let's play."

Aki and her new friend spent the next two weeks playing games, reading, and drawing pictures of themselves covered with red spots. For Aki, the quiet nights, when there was nothing to distract her, were the hardest. She tried to convince herself that nothing had changed, that she would go home to find Seiko and her parents sitting at their dining table.

But deep inside she knew it wasn't true. Once she recovered from the chicken pox, she wasn't going home. Her father wasn't waiting for her.

In the dark hospital room, Aki would think these things and cry silent tears, private tears, the kind that left no trace except for a wet spot on the pillow that dried before morning.

A nurse accompanied Aki on the long train ride out to Poston. Soldiers wearing tan uniforms and carrying duffel bags waited on the platform as the train pulled away.

They each have one bag, Aki noticed. *Only what they can carry.*

"Isn't this exciting?" the nurse said. "You'll be able to see your parents soon."

Aki nodded and gave a tight-lipped smile.

Not Pop.

The nurse reached for the *Saturday Evening Post* and soon settled into reading her magazine.

Aki gazed out the window, watching the lush green of the California growing country turn into the dry, dusty, bleak Arizona desert.

Who can live out here?

When the train pulled into the station, Aki hungrily searched faces in the crowd on the platform, looking for her mother.

Aki didn't trust her eyes at first. Her mother was standing on the platform weeping. Aki had never seen her mother cry in public before.

What has Poston done to her? Aki wondered as fresh fears crowded her imagination.

The train squealed to a halt, and passengers rose and began to collect their belongings. The nurse took Aki's suitcase in one hand and Aki's hand in the other, and together they made their way out into the crowd.

As soon as Aki saw her mother again, she broke free and rushed to her. They clung to each other, forcing the horde of strangers to flow around them.

She felt her mother's soft hands stroking her hair, and she let herself feel how much she had missed her.

Then Aki said good-bye to the nurse, picked up her suitcase, and took her mother's hand.

She missed her father.

She missed her home.

She missed the life she used to have.

But when she felt her mother's hand in hers, she knew that she was ready to face Poston.

CHAPTER 5

That which isn't in books, life will teach you.
—MEXICAN PROVERB

Sylvia
Westminster, California

Sylvia had looked all over the farm for her father before she finally found him behind the big barn. He was tuning the tractor engine with the help of Mr. Ortega, one of the men who worked for him. For weeks that big Allis-Chalmers Model B tractor had been sputtering and hacking, sometimes coughing out smoke until it stalled out completely.

"Mom says the other men have finished dinner," Sylvia said. "She wants to know if you want to eat."

"Okay," her father said. "We're almost finished here."

Mr. Ortega turned the key in the ignition, and the engine started up right away. It rumbled, loud but steady.

"It's the timing," Mr. Ortega said. "Hear that? Now she's nice and even, just the right mix of fuel and air."

Sylvia's father smiled. "I can't thank you enough," he said, closing the repair manual. "Please join us for dinner and then let me take you home. It's getting late."

About a dozen of the men who worked on the Mendez farm stayed in the farm's bunkhouse, but Mr. Ortega and several others lived in the barrio. He usually caught a ride with the other workers to and from the farm, but everyone else had already left for home.

After washing up, Mr. Ortega joined Sylvia's father at the dining room table in the main house. Sylvia's mother brought them each a large bowl of steaming *chile con carne*.

"I think my daughter, Sylvia, is in class with one of your children," Sylvia's father said after swallowing his first bite.

Sylvia was in the kitchen washing plates, but she perked up when she heard her name. She could just see Mr. Ortega from the sink.

"Don't your children go to Hoover School?" her father prompted Mr. Ortega.

"Pablo and Sonya go to school there," Mr. Ortega said, wiping the edge of his mouth with a napkin. "My oldest son, he is at Camp San Luis Obispo, Fortieth Infantry Division."

"You must be very proud of him," Sylvia's mother said, putting a platter of cornbread on the table.

"I am."

Sylvia knew what was coming next. Her father couldn't pass up an opportunity to try to convince the parents of Hoover students to sign his petition. Superintendent Harris had never followed up about switching Sylvia and her brothers to Westminster School, so her father had organized the *Asociación de Padres de Niños México-Americanos*—the Association of Parents of Mexican-American Children.

As her father talked about segregation in the schools—a term Sylvia was hearing a lot of lately— Mr. Ortega remained quiet, looking down at his chili.

"Separating our children by the color of their skin is wrong," her father said. "The children should go to school together. Don't you think so?"

Mr. Ortega glanced up at Sylvia's father, nodding in agreement, but indicating that his mouth was too full to speak. Sylvia, watching intently, suspected he didn't want to get into an argument with his host.

"So would you be willing to sign a letter to the school board?" her father asked.

Mr. Ortega swallowed. "Sign a letter? Oh, no, no," he said unhappily, shaking his head. "I can't do that."

"It's a simple letter," Sylvia's father explained. "It just asks for better schools."

"I don't want trouble," Mr. Ortega countered.

"I don't want trouble, either," Sylvia's father said reasonably. "But I want my children to get a good education."

Sylvia felt sorry for Mr. Ortega. *What could he possibly say to that?*

"Think about it," Sylvia's father said. "Your son is risking his life for his country, while his little brother can't go to school with his white neighbors."

"I know, I know," Mr. Ortega agreed, sounding miserable. "But we can't change the school system. If we complain, all we will get is trouble."

"I don't know about trouble," Sylvia's father answered, his voice sounding hard edged. "But I do know that we won't get anything if we don't ask."

For a few minutes an awkward silence separated the two men. At last Mr. Ortega murmured: "I'm sorry. I really am, but I can't."

Sylvia's father sighed. "I understand. I wish things were different, but I understand."

Sylvia's mother began gathering up the last of the dinner dishes. "Sylvia, help me clear the table, then finish your homework and off to bed."

Sylvia had so many questions, but she kept quiet and dutifully helped her mother carry the plates and silverware out to the kitchen.

The following morning at breakfast Sylvia asked her father, "Why wouldn't Mr. Ortega sign the letter?"

"He was afraid. So many people are afraid of challenging the school board."

"Why?" Sylvia asked.

"Some people worry that if they speak out for change they will lose their jobs or get sent back to Mexico. Some people want their children to go to Hoover School because it's near the barrio." He let out a heartfelt sigh. "The only life they see for their children is the life they have lived themselves: working at low-paying jobs, having children too young, never speaking up, being certain that the future can only be like the past."

Sylvia had grown accustomed to the routine at Hoover School. She had promised herself, *I will be the best student I can be, whatever school I'm in. I will make my parents proud of me.*

"Dad," Sylvia said, "Hoover isn't really so bad."

Her father froze with a forkful of *huevos rancheros* halfway to his mouth. "No," he said, turning toward her. "It *is* bad. At Hoover School, no one expects you to succeed, to finish high school, to go on to college. At Hoover School, no one thinks you can make something of yourself. They believe your future is in the fields.

"Sylvia," her father continued, "I want more than that for you. For all of you."

Sylvia flushed. She didn't know what to say.

"Don't sell your family short," he finished. "Don't sell yourself short."

Sylvia knew her father was right. At Hoover School the girls learned sewing and homemaking and the boys learned a trade like fixing cars; little time was devoted to reading and math and science. She knew for a fact that almost all of the students at Hoover dropped out before the eighth grade to work full-time in the fields or at low-paying jobs in town.

This was not the future Sylvia wanted for herself. Now she wondered: *Can I keep my promise to succeed in a school where no one really cares if I get good grades or find a good job?*

After weeks of trying to convince people to sign his letter to the school board stating that Mexican and white children should go to school together, Sylvia's father had collected only eight signatures.

"What are you going to do with the letter?" Sylvia asked her father. She didn't think he would turn it in with so few names.

"I'm going to deliver it," he said. "It would be the right thing to do, even if no one else is willing to sign."

Sylvia rode with her father to the courthouse in Santa Ana on the day he dropped off the letter. Just a couple of blocks from the courthouse Sylvia saw a sign posted in a diner window: NO DOGS OR MEXICANS.

The words made her feel sick. She was glad her father had spotted someone he knew on the street and hadn't noticed the sign.

That sign is talking about me, she thought. *Dogs and Mexicans and me.*

The sign gnawed at Sylvia all afternoon and into the evening. Before drifting off to sleep that night, she stared at the ceiling and thought about how those four little words could hurt her so much.

Then she recalled the hateful signs she had seen posted in town about the Japanese—hand-lettered signs reading JAPS GO HOME and government-printed notices telling them that they had to go away, to leave their houses, to go to the camps. This made her think of the girl she knew only from a photograph and the few scraps of her life that were left in what was now Sylvia's bedroom.

How did Aki feel when she saw those signs and read those posters? Sylvia wondered. *Did Aki feel as hurt as I do now?*

Sylvia looked over at her dolls. Carmencita leaned against the corner of one shelf, and Keiko stood in the corner of another.

Sylvia got out of bed and moved Keiko to the shelf next to Carmencita. She placed the dolls side by side, then stood back. *How nice they look together—almost like sisters.* She rested Keiko's pale china hand in Carmencita's brown cloth one. It seemed right and good to see them so close.

I wonder if I will ever meet Aki. Could we ever be friends?

CHAPTER 6

Adversity is the foundation of virtue.

—JAPANESE PROVERB

Aki

Poston, Arizona

Aki and her mother crowded onto a bus filled with other families riding to Poston from the train station. Most people were dressed in their best clothes—men in suits and fedoras, women in dresses with gloves and small hats that matched their overcoats. Children stood hand in hand with their parents, everyone somber and quiet.

On the bus ride, Aki took in the landscape. On either side of the road she saw nothing but desert, miles and miles of flat, dry dirt. Off in the distance, rugged purple mountains cut a jagged line along the horizon and looked just as unfriendly and desolate as the desert.

This is a lonely, awful place, Aki decided. She shifted closer to her mother on the seat beside her.

"Have you heard from Pop?" Aki asked.

"Not yet," her mother responded. "The post office isn't open yet. Soon. I know it will be soon."

As the bus approached Poston, Aki saw what looked like army barracks surrounded by a chain-link fence topped with barbed wire.

"Where are we?" Aki asked.

"The Sonoran Desert," her mother said. "Poston."

Aki felt relieved that her mother didn't say, "Home."

A uniformed soldier stood outside the front gate. He didn't carry a rifle, but he didn't need to.

Even if we did escape, where would we go?

The tiny blades of the barbed-wire fence glinted like silver shark's teeth in the sunlight.

Her mother whispered, "Whatever you do, don't go near that fence."

As they climbed off the bus, they were herded by guards through an administration building. When they exited on the other side they were inside Poston.

Aki tried to get her bearings. It wasn't easy, because everything looked the same—row after row of slapped-together wood and tar-paper structures resting on concrete bases. There were no trees or grass, just dust and dirt. They turned right, walked halfway down the street, and stopped in front of a house that was about a hundred feet long by twenty feet wide with four entrances.

"There are four rooms inside," her mother said. "For four families."

Four families live here? In this little space?

"Come inside," her mother said.

Aki climbed several wooden steps and entered a stuffy room furnished with steel-frame army cots, a table and chairs, a broom, a potbellied stove, and a coal bucket. Gray wool army blankets lay neatly folded at the foot of each bed.

Aki counted three beds: for Seiko, her mother, and her. *We'll need another bed for Pop when he comes back to us,* she thought.

More wool blankets hung from the ceiling, dividing the space into sections, one for each of the families. There were no real interior walls.

"Where is Seiko?" Aki asked.

"He's working," her mother replied. "He got a job as a carpenter. He's getting paid—and it gives him something to do."

Aki placed her suitcase next to one of the beds. She looked around the room and drew a deep breath. She didn't want to unpack her things. She wasn't ready to admit that this was to be her home, not yet.

"Could we go for a walk?" Aki asked. "Look around?"

"Of course," her mother said. "Sunshine will do you good."

A gray-haired woman with a straw broom was sweeping the next doorstep.

"Good afternoon," Aki's mother said. "This is my daughter, Aki, the one we have been waiting for." She turned to Aki. "This is Mrs. Fujioka. She is from Sacramento. Her daughter and grandson live here, too."

Aki nodded. "I'm pleased to meet you."

Mrs. Fujioka smiled. "Welcome."

Aki followed her mother on a tour of the residential blocks, the school, the administration buildings, and the canteen. Each building looked just like the next.

Will I ever be able to find my way around without a guide? she wondered.

As they walked, Aki looked for Yuki's face. "Have you seen my roommate from the hospital? She's here now, too."

"Oh, honey," her mother said. "This is a big place. There are thousands of people in three separate camps. You'll make lots of friends."

They stopped by the latrine. Aki stepped inside and saw to her horror that the bathroom was an open room. There was a raised platform in the middle with six holes and no walls.

No privacy!

When they were back outside, Aki said, "I don't like the bathroom."

"I know," her mother said. "I don't either."

Aki's mother pointed to a building up ahead. "Now I will show you the mess hall."

"Mess hall?" Aki asked.

"The cafeteria," her mother said. "The place where we eat."

Outside the mess hall, Aki spotted Seiko, who was waiting for them. He looked older. Aki squinted and, for just a moment, imagined that he was her father.

Seiko threw his arms around Aki and lifted her right off the ground. "Welcome home, little sister."

Aki didn't like what she heard. *How could this hot, dusty, cramped place, without Pop, ever be home?* But she just smiled and hugged him back.

Together the three of them entered the mess hall and lined up for dinner. Some people stood in a long line, waiting for food; others sat at rows of picnic tables eating their meals.

Every face she saw was Japanese: the infant smearing food across his face, the elderly woman wiping the corner of her mouth with a napkin, the teenage girl whispering to her laughing sister, the child sopping up a glass of spilled milk, the mother cutting her daughter's food, the father scolding his crying son.

"So many people," she said.

"They're from all over—Fresno, Monterey Bay, Sacramento," Seiko told his sister. "You'll get used to the noise."

They collected their food on battered metal trays, then sat together at the end of a table.

"What is this?" Aki asked, looking cautiously at the toast topped with flakes of dried beef in a white sauce.

"They call it chipped beef," her mother replied, unfolding a napkin in her lap.

"Get used to it, kid," Seiko said. "We have it a lot."

Aki took a couple of bites. The salty beef and thick white sauce felt heavy in her stomach. She wasn't used to eating such rich food. She longed for her mother's *harusame* noodle salad and steamed rice.

After dinner they returned to their unfamiliar room and Aki's mother helped her put her things away. She handed Aki a glass and motioned to a bucket near the door. "If you are thirsty in the night, this water is for drinking."

Later, when it was time to change her clothes, Aki stood in a corner, her back turned to the room. Seiko and her mother looked away. Without removing her dress, Aki pulled on her nightgown over her head. Hidden by her sleepwear, she unbuttoned her dress, wriggled free, and then slipped her arms into the sleeves of her gown. Although her body was covered the whole time, Aki felt her face redden, embarrassed by the lack of privacy.

Aki looked at the beds. "Would it be okay if we moved our cots closer together? *Kudasai?* Please?"

"Of course," her mother said. "I would like that, too."

Aki pushed her narrow cot next to her mother's, close enough that they could reach over and hold hands in the darkness.

"Mom." Aki pulled the sheet up to her chest. She kept her voice low and tried not to listen to the whispers coming from behind the blanket walls all around her. "I miss Pop."

Her mother brushed the hair from Aki's face. "I do, too."

"I don't like the food, but the rest isn't so bad."

"The beginning is easy," said her mother. "The continuing is hard."

Although it was not yet summer, at lunch she overheard one of her neighbors say that the temperature outside was more than a hundred degrees.

"That's nothing," Seiko said. "I've been told that the highs around here can reach a hundred and fifteen degrees or more in the summer."

Aki wanted to think he was kidding, but she knew he wasn't.

"The government calls Poston's three camps Poston I, II, and III," her brother said. "We call them Roastin', Toastin', and Dustin'."

She wanted to laugh, but it was too hot even for that.

When they got back to the room, Aki sat in the doorway and fanned herself with a copy of the *Poston Chronicle*, the camp newspaper written by the internees. Seiko and their mother stood outside, chatting with Mrs. Fujioka.

Out of the corner of her eye, Aki thought she saw something move inside the room. She turned around and saw a large black snake slithering up through a gap in the floorboards.

"Seiko!" she shouted. "A snake!"

In what seemed like one swift movement, Seiko grabbed the metal shovel next to the coal bucket and smashed the snake until it looked like a flattened rotten banana. When it stopped moving, he scooped it up and took it outside.

When he returned, Aki's heart was still racing. She smiled at her brother with admiration.

"What's a snake doing here?" she asked.

"He lives here," Seiko said. "We're the ones who don't belong."

Aki knew he was right. She and her family belonged at their farm in Westminster. She belonged in her room, on her bed, under her yellow cotton bedspread. She thought about the Mexican family that her mother said had leased the farm.

Was another girl living in her room?

Sleeping in her bed?

Going to her school?

I want to go home.

PART II

California and Arizona
1944–1945

CHAPTER 7

Do the good and don't look at who receives it.
—MEXICAN PROVERB

Sylvia
Poston, Arizona

"You better hurry up if you want to come with me," Sylvia's father said, smiling. For two years she had begged to ride with him when he went to the internment camp to deliver the rent payment to the Japanese family. This was the first time he had agreed to let her join him.

"Really?" Sylvia asked. "I can go with you?" She rushed to find her shoes without waiting for an answer. She didn't want to give her father a chance to change his mind.

A few minutes later Sylvia was in the Pontiac sedan and they were on their way. Sylvia's father asked, "What do you know about where we're going?"

"To the place where the Japanese family lives," she said.

"That's right," he said. "To Poston. And do you know what an internment camp is?"

Sylvia nodded. "It's a prison for Japanese people."

"Not exactly," he said. "The people there aren't prisoners. They didn't do anything wrong."

"Then why are they in there?"

Her father sighed. "It's complicated," he said. "Some people believe that the Japanese are a threat to our national security."

Sylvia didn't understand, but she didn't want to make him regret taking her along because she asked too many "why" questions.

They drove the 250 miles to Poston in four hours with the windows down and the radio on. Sylvia didn't often have the chance to be alone for so long with her father. She liked hearing him tap his hands against the steering wheel and the smell of his aftershave. She liked watching his dark hair flutter in the wind.

Along the way, just as the Andrews Sisters finished up "Boogie Woogie Bugle Boy," Sylvia asked, "Why don't you just mail the rent to them instead of driving so far?"

"It's up to me to make sure they get their money," he answered.

"Don't they get mail at Poston?"

"They do, but sometimes the censors who check the mail take things."

"They steal?"

"Some do," he said. "And the Munemitsus don't need excuses—they need their money."

Maybe the wrong people are locked up, she thought.

When Glenn Miller's "I've Got a Gal in Kalamazoo" came on, Sylvia settled back and listened to her father sing along. She closed her eyes and before long she fell asleep.

"There it is," her father said, waking her up. She could see in the distance what looked like clustered warehouses surrounded by a fence.

This place sure looks like a prison, she thought grimly, *no matter what Dad says.*

"Will I get to go inside?" Sylvia asked. "Can I meet the girl who had my room?"

"I have no idea," her father said. "We'll find out."

They left the car, went through security, and then waited in one of the administration buildings. After a few minutes, a Japanese woman, a young man, and a girl a little older than Sylvia stepped into the room.

The woman wore a plain cotton dress and her black hair was drawn into a neat knot at the back of her head.

"Thank you for coming," the young man said. The two men shook hands.

Sylvia's father placed his hand on her shoulder. "This is my daughter, Sylvia."

"*Hajimemashite*," the woman said, smiling and bowing slightly. "Nice to meet you, Sylvia. This is my son and my daughter."

"Nice to meet all of you, too," Sylvia replied.

Sylvia's eyes met the other girl's briefly. *That girl in the picture had shorter hair, but they have to be the same person,* she decided.

Her father handed Mrs. Munemitsu an envelope with the rent money, and then the adults began to discuss the farm's irrigation system.

"Is your name Aki?" Sylvia asked.

The girl's eyes widened. "Yes," she said. "How do you know my name?"

"You left your third-grade class picture in my closet—well, *our* closet," Sylvia said. "You wrote your name on the back."

Aki smiled. "Oh, yes; I remember."

"I'm staying in your room," Sylvia said. "The one with the yellow walls." Sylvia thought of it as her room now, but in her heart she knew that it also belonged to Aki.

Aki didn't say anything.

"When I first moved in I found your doll, the one with the red robe," Sylvia added. "It was on the high shelf in the closet."

"Her name is Miyoshi," Aki said.

"I didn't know," Sylvia said. "I call her Keiko."

"Keiko," Aki said. "I like that."

"I'll take good care of her for you."

Aki let out a sigh. Sylvia thought, *Maybe she doesn't like the idea of sharing her room. How frustrating it must be to stay behind that barbed-wire fence, watching us come and go.*

"Come along, Sylvia," her father said. "We need to get home."

Aki was looking at the ground.

I bet Aki wants to go home, too.

Before leaving, Sylvia marveled at how the people inside the camp had built an oasis in the desert. Between the barracks and in the fields around the buildings they had planted lush gardens and grown tomatoes, eggplants, squash, and other vegetables. In the two years they had lived there, the people of Poston had turned brown to green, barren to fertile, dead to alive.

They are farmers, Sylvia thought on the way home, *just like we are.* To the sun and the seeds and the soil, Mexican or Japanese, Mendez or Munemitsu didn't matter: the people knew how to make things grow.

CHAPTER 8

One kind word can warm three winter months.

—JAPANESE PROVERB

Aki
Poston, Arizona

"Shhh," Seiko whispered to someone as he shut the door. "Don't wake up my little sister."

"*Hai*, yes," another male voice said.

Aki felt a blast of frigid February air. Poston's cruel weather included both extremes: sweltering summers and winter lows well below freezing. The flimsy walls of the barracks did little to keep out either hot or cold.

Aki breathed slow and deep, pretending to sleep. Though she faced the wall, she had recognized the voice of Isohoi, her brother's friend.

"Are you going to fill it out?" Isohoi asked.

"I guess we have to," Seiko said.

Aki guessed that they were talking about the Leave Clearance Application, a questionnaire that had just been distributed to everyone at camp over age seventeen. Seiko had gotten one; he had recently turned eighteen.

"I don't know what they want us to say," Isohoi said. "I don't want to say the wrong thing in case it's some kind of trick."

"A trick?" Seiko asked.

"To test our loyalty."

"I haven't read it yet. Isn't it just a list of questions?"

"It's not that easy," Isohoi said. "Question twenty-seven asks if we're willing to serve in the armed forces of the United States on combat duty, wherever ordered."

Aki heard Isohoi slap some papers onto the table.

"I'm willing to serve my country," he said. "I'm willing to fight."

Then why not answer yes? Aki wondered.

"But not against Japan," the young man went on. "Not *in* Japan. My grandparents, my cousins, they still live there."

Aki understood: he might be fighting against his family. *How could this government—any government— ask such a terrible thing?*

"And if you don't answer yes," Seiko said, "then you're considered a traitor to the United States."

What kind of choice is that? Aki asked herself.

Cold blasted across the room again. Aki's mother had returned from the latrine.

"Isohoi," she said. "Good evening."

"It's late," Seiko said. "Let me read this over, and we'll talk about it in the morning."

Isohoi said good night and left.

Seiko sighed heavily. Aki heard him flip the paper over. At one point he slammed down the pen.

"Go to bed," their mother murmured. "We will talk in the morning."

Aki heard Seiko drop onto his bed. A moment later, he was back up, pacing the room.

What is the matter? Aki knew that her brother would not have to struggle with the question that bothered Isohoi. Seiko could not serve in the military. He had suffered from polio as a child and walked with a significant limp.

"This is wrong," Seiko said to his mother. "I am an American! How dare they ask me that!"

"Shhh . . . your sister. What is the problem?"

"Question twenty-eight." Seiko's voice was an angry whisper. "It says: 'Will you swear unqualified allegiance to the United States of America and faithfully defend the United States from any or all attacks by foreign or domestic forces, and forswear any form of allegiance or obedience to the Japanese emperor, or any other foreign government, power, or organization?'"

Seiko took a long breath.

"What nerve! I'm imprisoned in this camp, being denied my rights as a U.S. citizen, and at the same time I'm being asked to deny my loyalty to any other group."

Are we still U.S. citizens? Aki realized she didn't know.

"What am I supposed to do?" Seiko asked.

Aki felt sorry for her brother and torn in two herself. No longer fully American, yet not Japanese, either. Not quite a prisoner, not quite free. She felt lost in the desert, wandering between a past that was gone and a future that stretched before her, barren as the land surrounding them.

"You must do what you think is right," their mother replied softly.

Seiko sat at the table and filled out the form without another word. Aki could only hear the chair scrape the floor and his pen scratching the paper. Eventually he sighed heavily again, put down the pen, and returned to bed.

~

As May burned hot over Poston, Seiko lined up a job at a foundry in Denver as part of a work release program. He planned to save as much of his pay as possible so that the family would have money to start over when they were free.

Before her brother left Poston, Aki would have said that she could not possibly stand another separation. But she had been truly amazed to learn what her heart could bear when it had no choice but to keep on beating.

Aki and her mother accompanied Seiko to the administration building on the day he and about a dozen other young men left. She did not cry when Seiko said, "Well, I guess this is it." She did not cry when he hugged her and lifted her off the ground for what might be the last time for a long while. She did not cry when she heard her mother let out a whimper.

She tried to imagine a future, a not too distant future, when the war would be over and the entire family—she and Seiko and Mom and Pop—would be together again, when they would go back to the farm and things would be the way they used to be, the way they were supposed to be. That's all she could do these days, it seemed: just imagine and believe. And wait.

CHAPTER 9

God does not hear if you do not speak.

—MEXICAN PROVERB

Sylvia
Westminster, California

Painted on the side of Henry Rivera's yellow truck was a basket overflowing with fruits and vegetables and the words: RIVERA'S PRODUCE, SANTA ANA, CALIFORNIA.

"Hey, sweetheart," Mr. Rivera said when Sylvia entered the packing house where he and her father were talking. "How's the school year going?"

Before she could answer, her father interrupted, "Don't get me started with the schools." But Sylvia knew that he had already begun.

"Hoover isn't a healthy place for a serious student," her father continued. "They have outdated textbooks, overworked teachers, and a system that doesn't encourage Mexicans to go on to high school."

How many times had Sylvia heard this speech, word for word? In her mind, she recited along with her father the closing words: "It's unfair—it's an *insult*— that my children, all our children aren't allowed to go to their neighborhood school!"

Mr. Rivera looked thoughtful for a moment, then said, "I know a lawyer who specializes in integration cases. He's had a lot of success in Los Angeles."

"What's integration?" Sylvia asked.

"Integration means that you can go to Westminster, even if you're Mexican," her father replied. "It means that there isn't a white school and a separate Mexican school. It means there's one school and everyone gets the same chance to succeed."

"That's right," Mr. Rivera said. "David Marcus, the lawyer I'm talking about, he's won several integration cases. He's helped to integrate the public parks and pools in Los Angeles."

"What about schools?" Sylvia's father asked.

"I don't know," Mr. Rivera said. "But I do know that hiring any lawyer isn't cheap."

Sylvia could tell from the look on her father's face that he had already decided to hire the lawyer.

"It may be expensive," Sylvia's father said. "But the only thing more costly would be doing nothing."

On March 2, 1945, it was official: Sylvia's father sued the school system. On that date, attorney David Marcus went to the courthouse and submitted the papers for the case *Gonzalo Mendez v. Westminster School District of Orange County.*

For months Sylvia's father had left the day-to-day work on the farm to her mother while he and Mr. Marcus traveled around Orange County collecting evidence and lining up witnesses for the case. Sylvia's father often left the house before dawn and returned after dinner—sometimes putting in longer hours than he did when he worked in the fields. To make the lawsuit even stronger, Mr. Marcus filed the case on behalf of five parents—William Guzman, Frank Palomino, Thomas Estrada, Lorenzo Ramirez, and Sylvia's father—one parent from each of the five school districts in Orange County. This showed that the problem didn't exist only at Hoover School; there was discrimination against Mexicans throughout Orange County.

The school board had ignored Sylvia's father when he phoned the office and sent letters. But once he filed a lawsuit, Gonzalo Mendez had their attention.

A few weeks after the suit was filed, the phone rang as Sylvia and her family were sitting down to dinner. Sylvia's father got up to answer it.

"Good evening, Superintendent Harris," her father said, glancing over at the family and putting a finger to his lips to indicate that everyone should stay quiet.

Superintendent Harris is calling our home!

"I see," her father said. After listening for a while, he said, "Just my children or all of the children?"

The entire family waited motionless, straining to hear what was being said on the other end of the line.

"Are you asking me to drop the lawsuit?"

Sylvia could hear her mother's sharp intake of breath. Her father looked out the window toward the field.

"Yes, I understand," her father said finally. "But no thank you."

He waited a moment while Superintendent Harris spoke.

"There's really no need for my attorney to call," Sylvia's father said firmly. "I'm not interested." Then he hung up the phone.

He looked at the family and smiled as if he had just won the grand prize in the lottery.

"The school board decided to let you kids go to Westminster School after all," he said.

Sylvia's mother put her hand to her mouth in shock.

"We're changing schools now?" Gonzalo junior asked, confused.

"No," his father said. "You're staying at Hoover School for the rest of the year."

"Why?" Sylvia asked. "Isn't that what you wanted? For us to go to Westminster?"

"No," her father said, tilting his head and raising his eyebrows. "The lawsuit was filed for the benefit of all. This isn't just about you three anymore. It started out that way, but now it's about all five thousand Mexican students in Orange County."

"Every child deserves a chance," Sylvia's mother said.

Sylvia was stunned. All this time she had assumed that the lawsuit and all of the trouble was just about her and her brothers. Now, for the first time, she understood that something bigger was happening. Her father wasn't doing this just for his family: he was thinking about kids she would never meet, who went to schools she would never see.

Her father said, "Sylvia, there cannot be justice for one unless there is justice for all."

He returned to his seat at the dinner table, pulled up his chair, and reached for his fork, just as though nothing had changed. But to Sylvia, something *had* changed greatly.

It would have been easy for her father to accept the superintendent's offer and move them to the better school. But he didn't do that. He wanted his children to have the same opportunities as the children at Westminster—but he also wanted the other kids in the barrio to have the same opportunities that she and her brothers had. He really had filed that lawsuit "for the benefit of all." Sylvia had always known that her father was a good and fair man, but for the first time she realized that he was more than that.

"I think what you're doing is . . ." Sylvia searched for the right word. "Brave."

Her father nodded. "Thank you. Now let's finish dinner."

As the school year ended, thoughts of Westminster School were never far from Sylvia's mind. Her father's case would be heard on July 5. The evening before, the Fourth of July, Sylvia ran through the fields with her brothers, playing tag. Just before it got dark, her mother came out with a tub of homemade vanilla ice cream and bowls of strawberries and whipped cream.

When the sky darkened, her father gave the children sparklers that hissed and rained luminescent glitter down on their arms. Then he launched bottle rockets that shrieked through the summer air.

"Take a seat," he announced. "It's time for the grand finale."

Sylvia settled on a blanket next to her mother and gazed at the black sky, waiting. A moment later, her father lit a single fuse and stood back. A bright light streaked across the sky like a falling star before exploding high above them into thousands of tiny twinkles that gradually winked out of existence.

Sylvia gasped and her brothers clapped wildly.

"Do it again!" Jerome shouted.

"Nope," her father said. "That was one of a kind."

The blanket felt soft against Sylvia's head as she leaned back. She thought about Aki. *How does she celebrate a holiday that's all about freedom when she's inside an internment camp? What can the word* freedom *mean to someone trapped behind a barbed-wire fence?*

Sylvia said good night and went back to her room. She opened the stationery set she had received for Christmas and began to write Aki a letter. She wrote about school and her cat and her father's lawsuit. She tried to make the letter friendly and newsy, but that wasn't really the point.

This had been just about the most perfect summer night in Sylvia's entire life, and she didn't think it was fair that Aki had to miss it. Her letter might not bring any real comfort to the other girl, Sylvia realized, but she wanted Aki to know that someone was thinking about her.

CHAPTER 10

Love and a cough cannot be hidden.

—JAPANESE PROVERB

Aki

Poston, Arizona

Aki left the game of jacks she was playing with her friends when she saw her mother returning from the post office with three envelopes.

"Three letters!" Aki cried. "Three!" They had never received that many letters in one day before.

Aki's mother first opened the envelope that had been postmarked in Denver.

"It's from Seiko! It looks like it has something in it!" Aki said, hopping up and down. When Aki wrote to Seiko she always ended with the plea "Please send candy and gum!" and Seiko often enclosed treats with his letters.

"Just a minute," said her mother with a laugh. "Let me read the letter first." She opened the envelope and removed a sheet of paper.

Aki was *sure* there was a treat inside the bulging envelope.

Her mother shared the highlights: "Seiko bought a truck . . . a 1938 pickup, light blue . . . He doesn't drive much because gas is so expensive . . . They've had a lot of rain . . ."

"Anything for *me*?" Aki demanded.

"Hold on," Aki's mother said, turning over the last page. "Oh, yes. Your brother does have something for you."

Aki's mother reached into the envelope and handed her daughter a pack of Wrigley's spearmint chewing gum and a Hershey bar.

"Thank you!" Aki squealed with delight. She unwrapped a stick of gum, carefully folding the silver paper and slipping it back into the pack. In the camp she'd learned to waste nothing. She chewed the gum several times, then took a deep breath, allowing the spearmint flavor to create a cool, tingly sensation inside her mouth.

Aki's mother placed Seiko's letter back in its envelope. Next she opened the envelope stamped with PRISONER OF WAR.

"This one's from your father."

But Aki had known right away. She always cringed when she read those words on Pop's letters. *Why is he a prisoner of war?* she asked herself time after time. *He is not the enemy.*

Aki's mother carefully removed the letter. Once again it had been cut into ribbons. Aki's father tried to write in English, but sometimes he included a Japanese word or phrase when he didn't know how to express a thought any other way. Military censors cut the Japanese sections right out of the paper, just in case they included military secrets. At times her father's letters had so many holes in them that they reminded Aki of the paper snowflakes she'd once made in art class at Westminster School.

Aki's father always wrote her name several times so that she could spot it even in a shred of a letter. Even if nothing else in the letter made sense, her name did: he was thinking about her.

Aki's mother held out the final envelope. "This one is addressed to you."

"Me?" Aki asked, puzzled.

But she immediately recognized the return address: her own home in Westminster, California.

"It must be from Sylvia!"

Aki tore open the envelope and pulled out the letter—three pages filled front and back. Sylvia's stationery was light pink with a cluster of roses in the corner of each sheet. On the first page, in large, loopy script was: "Dear Aki, I promised I would write to you, so here I go."

Sylvia wrote about her teacher, who was so mean that she made kids sit in the corner facing the wall if they got caught speaking Spanish at school.

She wrote about her new kitten, Ginger, who'd earned her name both because she was the color of fresh ginger and because she moved as gracefully as Ginger Rogers, the movie star and dancer.

And she wrote about her father, who was going to court so that Sylvia and her brothers would be able to go to Westminster School. "My dad really, really wants us to get a good education," Sylvia wrote. "Sometimes it's hard, but I'm really proud of him."

On the last page, just after her signature, Sylvia had taped a short article from the newspaper: "Westminster Man Sues School System." The article even mentioned Sylvia and her brothers by name.

Wow, Aki thought, running her finger over Sylvia's name in the article. *Someone famous is living in our house, in* my *bedroom.*

Aki kept all of her letters in an old cigar box that a neighbor had given her. She saved everything that people sent her, every card, every envelope, every candy wrapper. Her mother had locked away the old photographs they'd brought with them, so these scraps were all she had to help her hold on to a normal life, and most of all to her father.

Sometimes, before she fell asleep at night, Aki looked through the box and tried to remember her father's face, but more and more he seemed a ghost to her now. She hadn't seen him in more than two years.

Aki was so different from the little girl he'd seen the morning he disappeared from her life. She now stood four inches taller and her hair hung eight inches longer than it had then. *If we were to meet, would we recognize one another?*

Aki remembered her father's smile and the gap between his two front teeth. She thought about how hard he worked, always the first out in the fields before dawn and the last to come inside at night.

She missed her father most on the camp's movie nights, when families sat together. Aki always sat next to her mother, but when the lights dimmed in the auditorium, she scanned the men in the crowd, searching for one who might be her father, just in case he was there in the dark looking for her, too.

One Friday afternoon she returned to the barracks after school, planning to tell her mother that she wanted to skip the movie. She just couldn't stand the thought of her father not being there yet another night.

As she approached the door, Aki heard voices inside. She didn't expect her mother to be home from her job in the camp kitchen until later.

Who is inside?

Aki found a man speaking quietly with her mother. It took a moment for her to see that the man sitting in a chair a few feet away from her was her father.

"Pop?"

Her father stood as Aki rushed to him and he folded her in his arms. Aki clung to her father so tightly that her arms began to tremble.

"I love you, Pop," she said when she found words.

"I love you, too," he said.

Aki had always known that her father loved her. He had shown her a million times in the ways that he took care of her. But that was the first time that Aki could remember him saying it in words.

"Please don't leave me," she said. "Please, don't ever leave me again."

Aki felt her father's embrace tighten. In the safety of his arms, anything—even an end to life at Poston—seemed possible.

"The war is winding down," her mother said. "We will be going home soon."

Home? It was almost too much to believe. Aki felt like she was on the brink of getting back what had been lost to her—her father, her home, her family, her whole life.

CHAPTER 11

*Talking about bulls is not the same thing
as facing them in the ring.*
—MEXICAN PROVERB

Sylvia
Los Angeles, California

Sylvia stood as Judge Paul J. McCormick entered the courtroom. She felt like she was in the principal's office and someone was going to be in a lot of trouble.

The judge wore a long black robe, like the graduation gowns she had seen in the newspaper. *Someday I will wear a graduation gown just like that,* Sylvia thought.

"Please be seated," the judge said.

Sylvia sat down, carefully tucking her dress under her to avoid wrinkles. She wore her favorite church dress, red and black plaid with a built-in petticoat, and her black patent-leather shoes, even though they pinched her toes. She wanted to look her best and make her father proud.

Sylvia noticed the court reporter, a young woman who sat up very straight and made her fingers fly across a strange keyboard device, typing out every word that was said. When there was a pause, her fingers rested; when someone spoke, her fingers came alive.

How can she stay focused, without letting her mind wander even for a minute?

Sylvia thought about the secretary in the Westminster School office, the one who had sent her away almost three years ago. *That's where all of this started,* she thought. *I wish Aunt Soledad didn't live so far away so that she could be here to see where that day has brought us.*

At first Sylvia's father's attorney, Mr. Marcus, and the lawyer for the school system took turns asking each other questions. Sylvia's father sat near them at the front of the room, occasionally speaking quietly to his lawyer. After what seemed like hours, no witnesses had yet been called to testify.

Sylvia whispered to her mother, "What's happening?"

Her mother cupped her hand around Sylvia's ear and whispered back, "The lawyers agreed that all the schools acted the same way. Instead of listening to all five school districts, they will hear from only one. Otherwise this case would last five times longer."

Sylvia nodded. *I couldn't stand that!*

Finally, a witness was called: James L. Kent, superintendent of schools in the Garden Grove School District, which was one of the five districts in Orange County. Hoover School was in his district.

Mr. Marcus asked: "Who decides which school the children will attend?"

"The Board of Trustees tells me to take charge of that part," Mr. Kent said.

"Now, is it a fact, sir, that the school board policy is that children of Mexican parentage shall attend Hoover School—"

"No, sir," Mr. Kent interrupted.

"—between the first and sixth grades?" Mr. Marcus finished.

"No," Mr. Kent said. "However, the policy does read that for Spanish-speaking students and students who need help, we have set up Hoover School."

"What do you mean by 'Spanish-speaking students'?" asked Mr. Marcus.

"Those children who come to school with a language handicap."

"That applies just to the Mexican children, doesn't it?" Mr. Marcus asked.

"So far, yes," Mr. Kent said.

Jerome swung his feet back and forth, kicking the edge of his chair, *bang, bang, bang.* Sylvia's mother put her hand on his knee and he stilled.

"Do you give the children any linguistic tests before you send them over there, or do you just select them because they are of Mexican descent?" Mr. Marcus asked.

"We give them a test by talking to them."

"And who gives that test?"

"Either the principal or myself," Mr. Kent replied.

That's not true! No one ever spoke to me. Seething, Sylvia muttered, "No!" under her breath. She felt a tap on her wrist and looked up at her mother, whose eyes said: *I know, I know. But be quiet.*

The lawyers discussed how it wasn't against the law to separate the Mexicans into different schools as long as the schools were equal.

Sylvia wanted to laugh. No one would consider Hoover School and Westminster School to be equal. *If the schools were equal, then white kids would go to Hoover.* Sylvia knew that would never happen.

The lawyer for the school system told the judge that having separate schools was good for the Mexican children because it allowed them to take "Americanization" instruction to learn American values and customs.

Americanization? Doesn't that mean to make someone an American who isn't one? Sylvia wanted to say that she was just as American as he was. She wanted to tell him she had spoken English her entire life, that she could speak two languages—English and Spanish—not just one.

Lots of the kids at Hoover School speak fluent English, Sylvia thought. *That lawyer doesn't know what he's talking about.*

Sylvia looked over at her father. *How can he be so calm? If he can do it, I'll try, too.*

"Are you saying that all two hundred ninety-two pupils who attended Hoover School last semester had language difficulty?" Mr. Marcus asked the superintendent.

"No," Mr. Kent replied.

"But you still kept them in Hoover School, is that correct?"

"Yes."

"Is that because of their Mexican ancestry?"

"Not necessarily."

"Well, what is the other reason?"

"Because of their location with respect to Hoover School."

"What other reason is there besides the location?"

"Their social behavior. We check into that."

"What do you mean by that, sir?"

"We mean that Mexican children have to be Americanized much more highly than our so-called American children."

"What do you mean by that?"

"They must be taught manners. They must be taught cleanliness. They aren't learning these things in the home."

"What are they not learning at home?"

"Well, the cleanliness of mind, manner, and dress. We need to teach them how to get along with other people."

How could he say that about someone? About me? Does he actually believe it?

Sylvia's mother shifted in her chair and breathed deeply, in and out, through her nose. Sylvia thought her mother wanted to stand up and yell at him as much as she did.

Judge McCormick frowned. Sylvia liked that about him. He didn't seem to care for what the superintendent was saying, either.

"And you find that Mexican children require all that extra assistance?" Mr. Marcus asked.

"Yes," Mr. Kent replied.

"You mean that without any special tests or examinations you can determine that an entire group of children needs that help?"

"Oh, no," said Mr. Kent, "we give tests."

"What kind of a test do you give the children to determine if they require Americanization?"

"We have a talk with the parent and with the child to see what their attitudes are, whether they can speak the English language, and whether they are adapted to going to school," Mr. Kent said.

"If a child speaks English, is clean in mind, manner, and dress, and lives near another school, would that make a difference?" Mr. Marcus asked.

Sylvia sat up straight. They were talking about her and other kids like her.

"Yes, it would make a difference," Mr. Kent said.

"Do you have now at least one Mexican child attending the white school?" Mr. Marcus asked.

"No, sir," said Mr. Kent.

Sylvia shrank down in her chair. She stared at her hands.

I am clean, she thought. *I am clean.*

The following morning, Sylvia braced for another long day in the courtroom. Sitting still and listening to the superintendent was more difficult than she had expected.

How can a man put his hand on the Bible and swear to tell the truth and then lie like that? Is he right? Is something wrong with me?

She paid special attention to parting her hair precisely before her mother braided it. She wanted to show Mr. Kent that she was clean and neat.

It didn't do any good.

Her father's attorney, Mr. Marcus, began the second day of the trial where it had left off.

"Please tell the court in what ways the Mexican children are not acquainted with personal hygiene."

"They have problems with lice, impetigo, tuberculosis," Mr. Kent said. "They have generally dirty hands, face, neck, and ears."

"Are all the children dirty?" asked Mr. Marcus.

"No, sir."

"How many of them are dirty?"

"I don't know. A large proportion."

Mr. Marcus flipped a page on his yellow legal pad.

"Now, Mr. Kent, do you believe that Mexicans are inferior to whites?"

"No, I don't."

"Well, as a matter of personal hygiene, you believe that Mexicans are inferior?" Mr. Marcus pressed on.

"Those with whom I have come in contact with in the schools are, yes," Mr. Kent said.

"Well, in Hoover School, how many of those two hundred ninety-two children would you say were inferior to the white race in personal hygiene?"

"Oh, I would say at least seventy-five percent."

Sylvia looked at her mother, whose eyes were narrow with anger. Her father was inspecting his fingernails.

Mr. Marcus went on.

"Mr. Kent, with respect to their ability to learn, is it your opinion that the Mexican children are inferior to the white children?"

"In their scholastic ability, yes," said Mr. Kent.

"What percentage of Mexican children are inferior to white children in their scholastic ability?"

"Seventy-five percent."

"Now, in what other respects are the children of Mexican descent inferior to the other children in your district?" asked Mr. Marcus.

"In their economic outlook, in their clothing, their ability to take part in the activities of the school," Mr. Kent replied.

"Do you believe that the white students are superior to the Mexicans in the respects and in the details that you have mentioned here?"

"Yes."

"And is that one of the reasons that they are being segregated?"

"Yes."

"That is all," Mr. Marcus said, dismissing the witness.

Sylvia wanted to go home. She didn't want to return to Hoover School. She didn't want to go to Westminster School. She just wanted to go home, climb into bed, and hide from the world.

CHAPTER 12

Continuance is strength.
—JAPANESE PROVERB

Aki
Poston, Arizona

Not long after Pop's return, Aki was walking down to the latrine when she noticed a strange tension in the camp. Usually her neighbor Mrs. Fujioka would be watering her tomatoes and whistling, with her little grandson playing in the dirt near her feet. But today she saw her normally cheerful neighbor huddled with other adults, whispering, hiding their conversation from the children and the guards. It was like that all along her route. No one paused to offer her a "good morning" or even a smile and a nod.

"What's going on?" Aki asked her parents when she returned to their room. "It's like everyone knows a big secret but I don't."

Her parents looked at each other.

"The United States dropped a very deadly bomb on Japan," her father said wearily. "A lot of people are worried about their relatives in Japan."

He held out a copy of the *Los Angeles Times,* dated August 7, 1945. The headline announced, ATOMIC BOMB HITS JAPAN.

"Where did it happen?" she asked.

"Hiroshima," her father replied.

"Do you know anyone there?"

"Kochi-ken is not far," he said. "Everyone knows someone not far."

Aki looked at the ground, allowing her father to think in silence about his former homeland and those he had left behind. Neither her mother nor her father had immediate relatives still alive in Japan, but Kochi-ken had been the first home for both of them.

From the other side of the hanging blanket that divided the room, Aki could hear a muffled sob.

Her mother whispered: "Mrs. Fujioka's family lives in Hiroshima."

"Are they okay?"

"I don't think so," her mother responded.

The mood throughout camp remained somber, and every morning when the newspaper appeared, Aki saw the adults huddle. Mrs. Fujioka and many others had tried to contact their relatives back in Japan, but Aki didn't know of anyone who had been able to get through.

What happened to the people in Hiroshima? Aki wondered. *Just how powerful was that bomb?*

Aki began to read the newspaper—at least the headlines—to understand what was happening. A few days later, the words on everyone's lips were "Nagasaki" and "more deadly than the first."

How long can this go on?

Less than a week later, on August 15, 1945, Aki read the most gigantic headline she had ever seen. The *Los Angeles Times* screamed, PEACE! in letters that took up almost half the front page. Another headline under that read: "Japs Accept Allies' Terms Unreservedly."

"Peace?" Aki asked her father. "Real peace?"

"Yes," he replied. "The war should be over soon."

"And then?"

"And then we'll be able to go home."

Aki felt numb. The day she had longed for was finally near, but at a tremendous cost: tens of thousands of people had died already and cities had been destroyed, but what stuck in her mind was a photograph in a magazine of tens of thousands of fish floating on the water in the Sea of Japan. They had been killed by radiation from the bombs. Aki couldn't get that image out of her mind.

That's not how I imagined peace would look.

Once again, they could take with them only what they could carry. This time Aki did not struggle with what to put into her suitcase. This time her few possessions fit easily, with plenty of room for the rag doll she'd had to stuff into her luggage when she first left home.

Aki looked back at the room where she had lived for so long, now empty except for what had been there when her family had first arrived: three beds, a table, chairs, the coal bucket, and the wool blankets.

"Are you ready?" her mother asked.

"I've always been ready," Aki replied.

She lifted her suitcase and followed her father and mother out of the building and toward the front gate. Along the way, they said good-bye to Mrs. Fujioka and a few other friends who were still preparing to leave. Then they crossed the threshold of the gate, and Aki felt free again.

CHAPTER 13

Hope dies last of all.
—MEXICAN PROVERB

Bad and good are intertwined like rope.
—JAPANESE PROVERB

Sylvia and Aki
Westminster, California

On the long drive from Poston to Westminster, Aki rode in the front seat of Seiko's light blue 1938 Chevy pickup. He had left his job in Denver to return with the family to the farm. She was squeezed between her brother on one side and her parents on the other, but she didn't really mind.

When they turned down their driveway, Aki marveled, "Everything looks the same."

They drove past the main house, which the Mendez family had leased until the end of the summer.

"It does," Aki's mother said. "Everything looks the way I remembered."

Seiko parked the truck in front of one of the smaller houses, where they'd be staying. Aki helped her parents unload the boxes from the back of the truck. Then, eager to explore and to remember, she asked, "Can I go now?"

"Of course," her mother said.

Aki began to run as fast as she could, through the rows and rows of green. She spread her arms out at her sides and let the feathers of the asparagus plants brush against her palms as she ran. With the sun directly overhead, there were no shadows to chase her.

Aki sprinted without looking back until she reached the end of a row, where she stopped, breathless. She bent over at the waist, slowly and deeply filling her lungs. When she stood up she found herself facing the back of her old, familiar house. Her bedroom window, the fieldstone pathway, the aquamarine hose coiled next to the back door—everything looked exactly as she recalled it.

A voice startled her.

"Aki?"

"Hi, Sylvia."

The two girls smiled shyly at each other.

"Why are you running?" Sylvia asked.

"Because I can," Aki said, grinning.

"Welcome home," Sylvia said, grinning back. "Do you want to see your room?"

Aki's heart jumped. "Oh, yes, please. If you don't mind."

"Come on." Sylvia took Aki's hand and led her through the house to the back bedroom.

Aki quietly let her memories return. The light yellow walls still warmed her like sunshine; the sheer white curtains in the window still breathed in and out with the breeze. Just being there, just standing in that space, made her feel like she was nine years old again, before the war had changed everything.

Aki saw that the dresser and bed were where she'd left them. She eyed the shelves next to the bed and the bookcase against the wall.

Sylvia knew what Aki was looking for.

"I'll get her for you," Sylvia said. She opened a drawer and pulled out Keiko and Carmencita. She handed the Japanese doll to Aki.

Aki took the doll in her arms. She ran her fingers over Keiko's soft hair and whispered, "I didn't think I would ever see you again."

Sylvia felt a warm feeling of satisfaction rising in her.

"*Arigatou gozaimasu*," Aki said. "That's Japanese for 'thank you.' You have no idea how much I missed her."

"I told you I'd keep her safe. Her best friend is Carmencita," Sylvia said, holding out the other doll. "And one of her new favorite foods is empanadas."

"What?"

"She told me she likes empanadas."

"A Japanese doll who eats empanadas?" Aki asked. "I like that."

"Me too."

For the rest of the afternoon, Sylvia and Aki built a dollhouse out of an old cardboard tomato box. They glued scraps of wrapping paper on the walls for decoration. They made doll beds and tables out of empty cereal boxes and used bottle caps as dishes. They cut a front door opening that was just the right size for Keiko and Carmencita to pass through.

On the space above the door frame Sylvia wrote "Home Sweet Home."

During the several weeks before Sylvia's family was to return to Santa Ana, Sylvia and Aki played together like best friends. They chased the chickens, played hide-and-seek, and took turns riding Missy, the swaybacked old mare. Aki taught Sylvia to fly by climbing the ladder in the barn loft and jumping off the edge into the piles of soft hay below.

One hot day, Sylvia asked, "Do you want to play beach?"

"How do you play?"

"Follow me," she said, and led Aki to the side of the main house.

"First we have to dig a good hole." The girls used old buckets to dig into the loose, sandy soil.

"Then you add the water." Sylvia dragged the garden hose around from the back of the house and flooded the hole with a steady stream of cool water. When the water level rose, the girls took off their shoes and dipped their feet into the pool.

"Just like the beach," Sylvia said.

"Except there are no waves," Aki added.

Both girls closed their eyes and turned their faces toward the sun.

"You know, it's funny how things turned out," said Sylvia.

"What do you mean?"

Sylvia chose her words carefully to fit the idea that had been taking shape in her mind. "Something really bad turned into good things."

Aki looked at her quizzically.

"I mean, if you hadn't been forced to leave, I wouldn't have been able to come here. And I never would have met you. And my father wouldn't have begun his lawsuit, which might help a lot of kids in school."

Aki thought about that.

"Does that make sense?" Sylvia asked. "Some good coming out of something bad?"

Aki nodded slowly. "I think I know what you mean. I guess it's like my pop says: sometimes if you move a little and look at something from a different angle, you might just see that thing in a whole new way. My being sent to Poston was bad. Nothing will ever change that. But yes, I can still see how some good came from it."

<hr />

"Hop in the car," Sylvia's father said the morning the Mendez family was to leave the farm. "We've got to get going."

Sylvia climbed in after her brothers and sat by the open window.

"Wait! Sylvia!" Aki called, racing up to the car. "I have something for you." Through the window she handed Sylvia a gift wrapped in red paper.

"What is it?" Sylvia asked.

"Something for you to remember me," Aki said. "Don't open it until you get to your new room."

Sylvia looked at the package and smiled. She knew what was inside.

"I left something for you, too," Sylvia said. "It's on your bed."

Sylvia's father started the car engine.

"Thank you," Aki said, stepping back from the car.

"Thank you, too," Sylvia replied, holding up her package.

The girls waved until the Pontiac sedan turned off the driveway and onto the main road.

Aki went inside the house and straight to her room—her room!—where she saw Carmencita resting on the middle of her pillow.

"This is perfect!" Aki said aloud, even though there was no one around to hear her.

In the car Sylvia settled back in her seat and let the wind blow her hair. Her father drove through town.

No one in the car said anything as they turned onto Seventeenth Street and drove past Westminster School.

This time Sylvia didn't bother to turn her head to admire the landscape. She didn't imagine writing her name in cursive on a worksheet, walking down the polished halls, or swinging from the monkey bars. Instead, she held her Japanese doll tight against her chest and kept looking straight ahead.

EPILOGUE

California
1955

There is no bad that something good
doesn't come from it.
—MEXICAN PROVERB

Sylvia
Santa Ana, California

"I'm so proud of you," said Sylvia's father. "So proud." He stepped back to admire his daughter in her graduation cap and gown.

"This is an important day," her mother said, straightening the red and blue tassel hanging down from Sylvia's square mortarboard.

"I know," Sylvia said. She knew that when she stepped on the stage, shook hands with the principal, and reached for her high school diploma she would be representing her entire family.

"You look so grown-up," her mother said. "You're such a beautiful young lady."

Sylvia hugged her mother. "Don't make me cry."

"Come on," her father said, taking her mother's arm. "Let's take our seats."

Just a few minutes later, the band played "Pomp and Circumstance" while the Santa Ana High School Class of 1955 entered the auditorium. Sylvia and her classmates marched through the crowd and filled the front rows.

After she took her seat, Sylvia admired her ring: gold with a faceted red stone and CLASS OF 1955 etched on the sides. Her long, thin fingers and neatly trimmed fingernails reminded her of her father's hands, always so clean. Thinking of him, she felt a touch of regret that he had never had a chance to wear a class ring of his own.

After the principal welcomed everyone, the class valedictorian took the stage.

"Fellow students, we are coming of age at a unique time in our nation's history," he said. "This is a time of unparalleled opportunity for students of every race and every color. One year ago, the United States Supreme Court, in the case of *Brown v. Board of Education of Topeka,* unanimously ruled that schools could no longer separate children by race. We—all of us—stand on the threshold of a new day. Equality in education is the first step toward equality in opportunity."

Sylvia felt her heart blossom with pride. "Equality in opportunity"—that was what her father had been fighting for. His lawsuit had focused on children in Orange County, but after he won, it inspired the governor of California to make school segregation illegal all over the state. The *Brown v. Board of Education of Topeka* lawsuit was a lot like her father's case, only it protected children all over the country.

"Each one of you has a mission in life," the valedictorian continued. "Your mission is not something you learn in school. It cannot be told to you by someone else. It comes from deep inside of you. It is the thing you have been put on this earth to do."

Sylvia thought back to the day she had been turned away from Westminster School because her skin was brown and her last name was Mendez. She looked left and right, at her classmates, and saw white, brown, and black faces.

My father helped to make this happen, she thought. *My father helped bring us together.*

In that moment Sylvia savored the full impact of what her father had done for her—no, not just for her, for Mexican students across California. Her father had taken a stand and made the world a better, fairer, and more just place. And all these years later, she and her classmates were reaping the rewards of his efforts.

You did it, Dad. You're *the one I'm proudest of today.*

After the speeches were over and the diplomas had been handed out, the principal turned to the audience and said, "I now present the graduates of the Santa Ana High School Class of 1955." As one, Sylvia and her classmates took off their graduation caps, tossed them into the air, and cheered.

AFTERWORD

A NOTE ABOUT THE MENDEZ FAMILY

Sylvia and her brothers did briefly attend Westminster School before the lawsuit and its appeal were finally resolved. After leaving the asparagus farm, the Mendez family returned to Santa Ana, California. Sylvia graduated from high school, attended California State University in Los Angeles, and became a registered nurse.

Gonzalo Mendez died of heart disease in 1964 at age fifty-one.

Felicitas Mendez, Sylvia's mother, lived until 1998, just long enough to see the groundbreaking for a new school in Orange County named the Gonzalo and Felicitas Mendez Elementary School in honor of their accomplishments.

In October 2007, a U.S. postage stamp was issued honoring the sixtieth anniversary of *Mendez v. Westminster*. In 2011, President Barack Obama awarded Sylvia the Medal of Freedom, the country's highest civilian honor.

A NOTE ABOUT THE MUNEMITSU FAMILY

The Munemitsu family stayed on the farm in Westminster for several years after the end of World War II. They invited a number of displaced Japanese families to stay with them and work on the land in the years after the internment camps closed.

"Even after the internment camps, my father still believed in the American dream," said Aki. "He wanted to help other families save money and start over. He did not believe in self-pity."

Japanese Americans lost an estimated $200 million when they were forced into the camps. Some of them recovered a small part of their financial losses through the 1948 Evacuation Claims Act and another redress payment through the Civil Liberties Act of 1988, which provided an official apology and payment of $20,000 to each surviving internee. The Munemitsu family received their payment and donated the entire sum to the Japanese-American Museum in Los Angeles.

Sylvia Mendez and Aki Munemitsu both live in southern California. They lost touch with each other for years but were reacquainted as adults and remain friends to this day.

THE END OF SCHOOL SEGREGATION IN AMERICA

On February 18, 1946, almost one year after *Gonzalo Mendez v. Westminster School District of Orange County* was filed, Sylvia's father won his lawsuit. Much of the courtroom dialogue used in chapter 11 of this book is drawn almost verbatim from court records. The judge in the case, U.S. District Court Judge Paul J. McCormick, ruled that Mexican children in Orange County, California, had the legal right to go to school with white children.

More specifically, the judge ruled that California law did not allow local governments to create "Mexican" schools. In his written opinion the judge held that segregation—in this case, separating students by race—"fosters antagonisms in the children and suggests inferiority among them where none exists." In other words, having separate white and Mexican schools was unfair and wrong, and with the judge's decision it became illegal in Orange County, California.

The school board didn't accept the judge's ruling. On December 10, 1946, the attorney for the school board filed an appeal to the U.S. Court of Appeals for the Ninth Circuit in San Francisco. He hoped that the higher court would agree with the school board and overrule the lower court's decision.

During this time, the United States was going through a period of great social change. Before World War II, most people accepted the separation of people by race. After the war, Mexicans, African Americans, and other people of color questioned the fairness of racial segregation. After all, brave men and women of all races had fought together and risked their lives to protect freedom and democracy on the other side of the world. When they got home, they wanted to be able to enjoy the same privileges as everyone else.

Some people feared racial integration. They justified school segregation by arguing that the schools were "separate but equal." Many children like Sylvia Mendez knew from experience that separate rarely meant equal.

In the mid-1940s, many civil rights lawyers were looking for a lawsuit that could be used to overturn what was known as the "separate but equal doctrine." Some attorneys thought that *Gonzalo Mendez v. Westminster School District of Orange County* might be the case to do it.

One of the attorneys watching the Mendez case was Thurgood Marshall of the National Association for the Advancement of Colored People (NAACP).

He and several of his coworkers filed friend-of-the-court arguments in the appeal of the Mendez case, arguing that separate but equal was inherently unjust. (Additional friend-of-the-court briefs were filed by the American Civil Liberties Union, the National Lawyers Guild, the American Jewish Congress, and the Japanese American Citizens League.)

The school board lost the case. On April 15, 1947, the seven judges of the Ninth Circuit Court of Appeals in San Francisco unanimously affirmed the lower court's decision. While the court ruled in favor of Mendez, it used another legal argument that did not address the question of race or the legality of the "separate but equal" doctrine.

In response to the case, the state of California reviewed its own policies involving race and education. School segregation in California officially ended in June 1947 when Governor Earl Warren repealed all state laws that separated schoolchildren on the basis of race, ethnicity, or language. Children of all races could finally attend school together in California.

The Mendez case had an impact nationwide. Families in other states also wanted the best possible education for their children. After the Mendez case, similar lawsuits were filed—and won—in Arizona and Texas.

The Mendez case also influenced the landmark lawsuit *Brown v. Board of Education of Topeka,* which made school segregation illegal nationwide. In 1954, Thurgood Marshall filed a lawsuit involving a young African American girl who wanted to attend an all-white school seven blocks from her home, instead of an all-black school a mile away. This was the case that would change history, and Thurgood Marshall used many of the same legal arguments he had tested in the brief he first wrote for the Mendez case.

In an interesting coincidence, Earl Warren, the man who banned legal segregation in schools when he was Governor of California, went on to serve as chief justice of the U.S. Supreme Court. He presided over the Court when Thurgood Marshall argued the *Brown* case, and he wrote the unanimous 1954 U.S. Supreme Court decision that struck down school segregation across America.

While it was the *Brown* case that ended segregation nationwide, many people refer to the Mendez case as the "*Brown v. Board of Education* for Mexicans."

JAPANESE INTERNMENT CAMPS

During World War II, more than 120,000 people of Japanese descent living on the West Coast of the

United States were held in internment camps. They were imprisoned—many of them for years—even though there was no evidence that they had done anything wrong. They were never charged with any crime; they never faced a jury of their peers.

The first major step in this massive internment program began on February 19, 1942, a few months after the bombing of Pearl Harbor, when President Franklin D. Roosevelt signed Executive Order 9066, creating wartime internment camps to hold Japanese Americans and Japanese immigrants. One month later, the president signed another executive order authorizing the "relocation" of all people of Japanese ancestry. This order applied to both Japanese citizens living in the United States and American citizens of Japanese descent.

The federal government quickly built ten relocation camps, most in the Southwest. The facilities were hastily constructed and lacked privacy. Some of the early residents at the camps were forced to build the barracks and facilities for those who would come after them. The first of the camps, Manzanar, opened on March 22, 1942.

At first the internment program focused on "suspected enemy aliens," especially male immigrants who were leaders in the Japanese community, such as Buddhist priests, Japanese-language teachers, and newspaper editors. People who owned land, such as the Munemitsus, were also considered high risk. In the following months, the internment camps were filled with women and children.

At Poston, as at the other internment camps, an economy developed. The War Relocation Authority paid $19 a month to professionals, such as medical doctors, who worked in the clinics; $16 to skilled workers, such as masons or bricklayers; and $12 to unskilled workers, such as Aki's mother, who worked in the kitchen.

Despite their treatment, the vast majority of Japanese Americans remained loyal to the United States. During World War II, thousands of Japanese volunteered for military service. During the war, some thirty-three thousand Japanese Americans fought for the United States, including the celebrated men of the 100th Infantry Battalion and the 442nd Regimental Combat Team, who together became known as the "Purple Heart Regiment" for their sacrifices. By the end of the war, these groups had earned 18,143 individual awards of valor, becoming "the most decorated unit for its size and length of service in the history of the United States."

On January 2, 1945, President Roosevelt repealed the executive order establishing the internment camps. The mass evacuation program happened again—this time in reverse—as families were released from the camps. The final internment camp, Tule Lake, was closed in March 1946.

In the final accounting, only ten people were convicted of spying for Japan during World War II—and all of them were white. Not a single Japanese American citizen was found to be disloyal to the United States.

FURTHER READING

Bridges, Ruby. *Through My Eyes*. New York: Scholastic, 1999.

Cooper, Michael. *Remembering Manzanar: Life in a Japanese Relocation Camp*. New York: Clarion, 2002.

Denenberg, Barry. *The Journal of Ben Uchida, Citizen 13559, Mirror Lake Internment Camps*. My Name Is America series. New York: Scholastic, 2004.

Donlan, Leni. *How Did This Happen Here?: Japanese Internment Camps*. American History Through Primary Sources series. Chicago: Raintree, 2007.

Fleming, Maria, ed. *A Place at the Table: Struggles for Equality in America*. New York: Oxford University Press, 2002.

Good, Diane. *Brown v. Board of Education*. Cornerstones of Freedom series. New York: Children's Press, 2007.

Hoose, Philip. *Claudette Colvin: Twice Toward Justice*. New York: Farrar, Straus & Giroux, 2009.

Houston, Jeanne Wakatsuki, and James Houston. *Farewell to Manzanar: A True Story of Japanese American Experience During and After World War II*. New York: Bantam Books, 1983.

Kent, Deborah. *The Tragic History of the Japanese-American Internment Camps.* From Many Cultures, One History series. Berkeley Heights, NJ: Enslow, 2008.

Levine, Ellen. *Freedom's Children: Young Civil Rights Activists Tell Their Own Stories.* New York: Putnam, 2000.

Michelson, Maureen, and Mary Matsuda Gruenewald. *Looking Like the Enemy: My Story of Imprisonment in Japanese-American Internment Camps.* Troutdale, OR: NewSage, 2010.

Mochizuki, Ken. *Baseball Saved Us.* Illustrated by Dom Lee. New York: Lee & Low Books, 1995.

Sakurai, Gail. *Japanese American Internment Camps.* New York: Children's Press, 2007.

Thomas, Joyce Carol, and Curtis James. *Linda Brown, You Are Not Alone: The* Brown v. Board of Education *Decision.* New York: Hyperion, 2003.

Tunnell, Michael, and George Chilcoat. *The Children of Topaz: The Story of a Japanese-American Internment Camp, Based on a Classroom Diary.* New York: Holiday House, 1996.

BIBLIOGRAPHY

COURT RECORDS OF INTEREST

Plessy v. Ferguson. 163 U.S. 81, 63 S. Ct. 312 (1896).

Mendez v. Westminster, 64 F. Supp. 544 (S.D. Cal. 1946).

Mendez v. Westminster, 161 F. 2d 774 (9th Cir. 1947).

Brown v. Topeka Board of Education, 347 U.S. 483 (1954).

Documents and records of *Mendez v. Westminster* (1946) can be found at the National Archives and Records Administration, Pacific Region (Riverside), 23123 Cajalco Road, Perris, California, 92570-7298, (951) 956-2000.

Documents and records of *Mendez v. Westminster* (1947) can be found at the National Archives and Records Administration, Pacific Region (San Francisco), 1000 Commodore Drive, San Bruno, California, 94066-2350, (650) 238-3488.

Additional materials are housed at the Department of Special Collections and University Archives, collection number M0938, Stanford University Libraries, Stanford, California, (650) 725-1022.

BOOKS

Gonzalez, Gilbert. *Chicano Education in the Era of Segregation*. Philadelphia: Balch Institute Press, 1990.

Hayashi, Brian Masaru. *Democratizing the Enemy: The Japanese American Internment*. Princeton, N.J.: Princeton University Press, 2004.

McWilliams, Carey. *North from Mexico*. New York: Greenwood Press, 1968.

Moreno, Jose F., ed. *The Elusive Quest for Equality: 150 Years of Chicano/Chicana Education*. Cambridge, Mass.: Harvard Educational Review, 1999.

Murray, Alice Yang. *What Did the Internment of the Japanese Americans Mean?* Historians at Work series. New York: St. Martin's, 2000.

Strum, Philippa. *Mendez v. Westminster: School Desegregation and Mexican-American Rights*. Lawrence: University Press of Kansas, 2010.

Wollenberg, Charles. *All Deliberate Speed: Segregation and Exclusion of California Schools, 1855-1975*. Berkeley: University of California Press, 1978.

ARTICLES

Arriola, C. "Knocking on the Schoolhouse Door: *Mendez v. Westminster,* Equal Protection, Public Education, and Mexican Americans in the 1940's." *La Raza Journal* 8, 2 (1995).

Harders, R., and M. N. Gomez. "A Family Changes History: *Mendez v. Westminster*: Fiftieth Anniversary Commemorative." *Harvard Educational Review,* April 25, 1998.

McWilliams, C. "Is Your Name Gonzalez?" *The Nation,* March 15, 1947.

Ruiz, V. L. "We Always Tell Our Children They Are Americans: *Mendez v. Westminster* and the California Road to *Brown v. Board of Education.*" *College Board Review* 200 (Fall 2003).

FILM

Mendez v. Westminster: For All the Children/Para Todos los Niños. Written and produced by Sandra Robbie, KOCE-TV, Huntington Beach, Calif., 2002.

INTERVIEWS

Sylvia Mendez, personal interview, August 2005, as well as multiple telephone interviews.

Aki Munemitsu, personal interview, August 2005, as well as multiple telephone interviews.

PHOTOGRAPHS

Sylvia, age ten

Aki, age twelve

ACKNOWLEDGMENTS

Special thanks to my agent, Sarah Davies of the Greenhouse Literary Agency, for believing in me; and to my dedicated editor, Nicole Geiger, for believing in this project. This book wouldn't have happened without the two of you.

WINIFRED CONKLING studied journalism at Northwestern University and received her Master of Fine Arts in writing for children and young adults from the Vermont College of Fine Arts. She has written more than 30 adult nonfiction books. *Sylvia & Aki* is her first work for children. Winifred Conkling lives in northern Virginia.